Totally Bound Publishing books by Landra Graf

Full Throttle Cyborgs

DRAG ME DOWN

LANDRA GRAF

Drag Me Down
ISBN # 978-1-80250-771-3
©Copyright Landra Graf 2024
Cover Art by Erin Dameron-Hill ©Copyright April 2023
Interior text design by Claire Siemaszkiewicz
Totally Bound Publishing

Published in 2024 by Totally Bound Publishing, United Kingdom.

DRAG ME DOWN

Dedication

To Kayla, Mandy, Renee, Michelle and Roxy.
This one is for you!

Chapter One

Dakota 'Drag' Michelson had always believed in two things. The first was that good always triumphed. Today was no exception.

"Full Throttle has cemented themselves in Wespero history by qualifying for a regional trial race — not once, but twice!" Snapper roared over the crowd gathered in the Watering Hole, hoisting a large mug of house brew in the air with his cybernetic hand. The metal gleamed in the low light of the room. Drag's second-in-command stood on the small stage, a plywood platform that lifted folks about a half a foot off the ground and typically hosted music acts.

"They said we wouldn't be capable of staging a repeat, but our fearless leader… Drag!"

Everyone looked at him. Over a hundred pairs of eyes were staring him down and had pinned him in place like a goosemert caught in the act of burrowing. His feet were locked to the floor by a silent fear that made it impossible for him to move as he leaned against the bar. He'd never been big on attention, afraid they might find a flaw in his abilities. He managed to lift his own mug in acknowledgment.

A deafening cheer erupted throughout the room. Drag closed one eye as the noise hit his audio cortex just right to send a screech through his entire body, as if the sound had triggered an adverse reaction to the nanites in his system and his nerves were revolting.

"Drag has led us to front-pole position," Snapper continued between drinks. "Just as he has since the moment we voted him leader of Frog Lick, leader of our gang. We celebrate tonight to remember how far we've come, because tomorrow, after we win, we start working toward the championship!"

Another roar rose through the room, paired with the clinking of glasses, the guzzling of brew and a jovial mood that no one could erase. This was the release of years of suffering. This gang had fought and clawed their way through poor engine designs, bad luck, explosions and losing their chance at an appeal with the Mars Shipping Commission.

No amount of presented evidence could convince that three-person board to commute or reduce the sentence they had handed down to Frog Lick three years prior, all courtesy of Bebe Smith, the previous gang-town leader, who'd been in a dirty deal with a terrorist cell from Earth's moon. She and the terrorists had almost launched an attack on the Uppers that would have made all of Mars suffer. The ruling groups of Mars had meted out the steepest punishment they could to show the APU that they wouldn't let treason on such a scale happen again. But did Bebe suffer? No... She got locked away in a prison cell and fed. It was the people she left behind who ended up worse off.

Hardworking women, men and their children had endured lack of food, support and, in some cases, much-needed medicine. They'd trusted Drag and his close friends to help lead the way and direct their efforts.

Their labor, sleepless nights and even repeated losses had been worth it to inspire them to reach this moment. The town had even flourished, becoming the place of his childhood dreams. No one went hungry. Not a single person froze because they didn't have proper housing. Everyone who wanted to learn was allowed to. There were no longer gender lines for jobs.

Drag dared a glance at Gaia, their bartender and another close confidant. Her long pale blonde braids were wrapped up in twin buns at the back of her head. She wore a smile that didn't quite meet her light gray eyes as she filled more mugs with brew and handed them off to one of the staff to distribute.

As if his stare had called to her, she sauntered in his direction. "You're pretty quiet for a man who should be on top of the world. Tomorrow is just a formality."

"We're not finished until we win the championship." They had put him in charge, expecting him to lead them to a future where their social standing or parental bloodlines didn't matter. For that, they needed to acquire the top reward gifted to gang-towns across Mars.

"Spoken like a man whose job is never finished. What then? When you win, how do you guarantee future success?"

He chuckled before swallowing a good amount of brew. "That's a problem for future me. Maybe you're right. I should be celebrating."

"Not a bad idea, considering we don't know what's on the horizon." Her words were soaked with the unspoken issues Full Throttle was dealing with outside of their win today. They were still without mining and shipbuilding rights and on the brink of a turf war with a rival gang.

That woman will do anything to bury me.

The memory of bright red hair, sizzling green eyes filled with hatred and a physical touch that still seared his skin... He'd exorcised her plenty of times from his mind, sometimes with a body and other times with booze. Tonight he'd have to do more of the same.

"Care to keep a man occupied?"

Gaia winked. "You know I don't mind a good spearing, but I've got other plans for tonight."

Drag didn't miss the bartender's gray gaze traveling across the room to a black-haired woman with bright eyes and winsome smile. Also, a nice set of tits.

"Well, if you need a third —"

"I'll remember you, oh fearless leader. How about you interact with the people? I bet they'd love a rendition of the drive or any kind word about how you'll be leading us to victory." With that, Gaia left him alone and he was back to staring out among the crowd.

Snapper had come off the stage to be replaced by Privy, their local musician, who had already started to tune up his guitar and prepare to strum. Music would fill the room soon enough and give Drag a chance to slip away.

He turned around and leaned over the bar, rummaging with his human hand for a bottle of the good stuff Gaia kept below. Emerging with an amber-filled bottle, he let out a little grunt of appreciation for the finer things, and for this moment.

"Did you ever think we'd be here? Two years ago, stumbling across the shitty terrain, outlawed, outcast and both with absent right arms." Snapper's voice brought a grin to Drag's face.

The idiot was already three sheets to the breeze. He'd been celebrating the minute Drag had finished the pole-positioning challenges.

"Either your woman's going to have no use for you because you'll be too drunk to get it up or too annoyed with all your reminiscing about the good old days. Hell, I'll have no use for you in the pit tomorrow." Drag had already spent enough time in his head about the past today. He'd rather use the rest of celebration to forget.

"Don't talk about Gina like that. She can get me up any time, booze or not. My woman is the best."

"You're damn right."

Snapper pointed a cybernetic finger in his face. "Don't you forget it. Now I may have drunk too much, but damn it, I'm in a good mood. We deserve a win, right?"

They did. The music started, a bawdy jingle about racers and the dust honeys who loved them. The crowd cheered and some even joined in. The lyrics were well-known and easy to recite. This right here couldn't be found elsewhere, not with any other gang.

Born wild and unafraid.
A mechanic by trade.
Raised to sweat in a driver's seat.

"Yes, but more than that, these people deserve the future we're trying to give them."

Snapper clapped a hand on his shoulder. "You're fucking right. I'm off to dance. Join us soon, don't wallow."

Drag tugged the stopper out of the bottle with his teeth, abandoning his now-empty brew glass and opting to tag a swig straight from the bottle. Another swallow, another verse.

He's known by all others.
A friend and brother.
Living for the thrill to compete.

The song and the booze were doing their job. Though he recalled another night this song had played, a time when he'd thought his path was headed in a different direction. One where he wouldn't be alone in his bed every night.

"Brother." Rune's voice was in his ear. Drag slapped the bar with his other hand in shock. He'd been so lost in his thoughts he hadn't seen Rune. His younger brother was a skinny, tanner and far nicer version of him. The kid had a wicked mind too, for agriculture and farming. He'd single-handedly helped Frog Lick avoid starvation after they had lost their primary source of income the last couple of years.

"Come to give me a hard time about joining the celebration as well?" Drag could always count on Rune to hand things to him straight. His brother wasn't afraid to tell him when he might be pushing too hard or making a bad decision. Like Gaia and Snapper, Drag relied on Rune to be a voice of reason during his time as leader.

"I'm here because you have a visitor."

Drag smiled and downed another good gulp, letting the burn coat his throat. "Tell them to join the party."

"Afraid that might bring more eyes to a situation we don't want attention for. Might encourage you to stop downing that whiskey like recycle."

"Who the hell's out there? The commission?" Hell, their racer had passed all the tests. Gina had triple-checked everything, including their NiteOx conversion that made sure to follow all regulations. "If they're here to accuse us of cheating, tell them it's too late."

Rune leaned in and whispered in Drag's ear. "It's Bridget."

Drag immediately sobered and the glass of the bottle cracked in his hand, whiskey seeping out through the edges over his skin, cool and wet. "Where is she?"

"Outside. She wants to talk. To parlay, is what she said. Said you know what she meant, but I believe her. She has that Inccukai assassin with her, no entourage."

Drag also believed no good deed went unpunished. So of course that bitch would show up now, during his moment of triumph. *She's a damn leech.*

"If I'm not back in one hour, get everyone outside and prepared for a fight."

"Are you sure that's a good idea?" Rune asked as he grabbed hold of the bottle in Drag's hand. "You can release the bottle."

"Good idea or not, if I'm not back, that means I'm dead or she is. Just be ready."

No interaction between them since that fateful day tended to end without someone injured. The one conversation with Hemi present had been an exception. From the moment she'd betrayed him, this was the way things had gone. The question was why the hell had she chosen to show up now?

* * * *

Bridget Macintosh had come for one reason. Now, as she stood waiting in this metal-roofed and walled shack, she couldn't help but consider this might be a trap.

"How did you get out of here before?" she asked the Inccukai who was blending in with the shadows against the far wall. They were near undetectable except for their eyes, bright red irises that peered at her from the dark.

"There's a dug hole in the corner, covered by a plate. I made it myself, though this building is used a lot more than when I first created it."

The implication was clear—the Inccukai had been spying in Frog Lick long before they'd been installed as a personal bodyguard for Bridget by her gang-town sponsor. *More like a spy for my own deeds.*

Bridget knew every move she made, any word or action, was shared with their sponsor via the hired assassin. Often Bridget had to exaggerate her reactions to display the kind of ferocity her gang had come to expect. Similar to what her sponsor wanted as well.

The fire, the anger and damn it... She clenched her fists tight and rolled her shoulders a couple times. *I'm still angry.* Pissed off that she was anxious about seeing Drag again. Hell, the last time they'd exchanged words, he'd threatened her.

"I've got the tape. Looks like you bribed a commission official for access to our area. The proof is mine, and all I need to do is expose you."

An error on her part—the very killer in the corner meant to protect her was supposed to have gotten rid of that physical evidence instead of leaving it on a hard drive hooked up to their mainframe. Proof the Inccukai had been cataloging ways to get her so wrapped in she wouldn't be able to get out.

She'd wanted to scream at Drag about how she'd had no choice, rail at him so he'd understand how she was forced to do whatever the bastard she'd allied with wanted, especially if it meant keeping the food supplies coming in to feed the gang and the contacts who wanted ships to increase the profits. Profits the sponsor took as much as he gave supplies in return.

I need him to see the mess he left me with.

Because it was his fault. She wouldn't be in this situation, vulnerable, alone and forced to do what she'd sworn she'd never do if he hadn't left her. He could have stayed in Macintosh gang, helped them rebuild after her father's death and claimed everything he'd earned. Moag Cheatham, her sponsor, had asked her for one thing in return and Drag had chosen to believe Snapper over her.

She'd always been left behind or put second. Even now, knowing that Cheatham was working against her, she had to come up with a better plan. A way to do something for herself. While she might stand here and consider begging Drag for his help, getting his agreement would be near impossible. She'd come to this drastic decision amid finding out her time as leader of Macintosh was numbered, that the one person who would do anything for Bridget was Bridget.

I'm going to save my own damn self.

The door at the front of the building swung open and she heard Drag before she saw him.

"I thought you said she was waiting outside the Watering Hole. This is down the street and you should really be putting her—"

"Hello, Drag. Congratulations."

He was swathed in shadows. She could barely see his face, just the corner of that strong chin of his, covered in scruff, paired with a strong bulky shoulder. "Fuck this. I'm going back."

The Inccukai moved like a damn puff of smoke from the corner to blocking the door. Drag hadn't entered alone. His younger brother Rune, who Bridget had approached first, stood right behind him.

There were about ten steps between Rune and the Inccukai.

"Joseph's balls! What the hell is that?" Rune shouted.

Drag sighed. "Her little hired weapon. Looks like we can't leave."

Drag closed the distance between them by half and that was when she got a good look at him in the low light. His eyebrows were hunched, his gaze damn near predatory and she didn't miss the way his jaw was clenched. "Give me one reason why I shouldn't choke you to death with this metal monstrosity of an arm I have."

"A Mars Shipping Commission appeal."

"Rune, wait with Bridget's killer outside."

Rune clucked his tongue. "I told Petal I would — "

"Ten minutes, that's it. I give her a few to explain herself and then she's out the door." Drag cracked the knuckles on his human hand one at a time.

"How do I know I'll be safe?" Bridget had to ask — she had only seen Drag do such a thing right before he threw a punch.

Drag grinned. "You don't, but I'm sure that assassin of yours will kill me quick if I touch a hair on your head."

"Wait outside, Trio."

"Funny, the creature has a name," Drag replied with a smirk. The idiot seemed to want to bait himself into a fight.

The Inccukai pushed open the door first, holding it for Rune to follow, which he did after exchanging glances with Drag. Trio didn't go right away. No, they waited for Bridget to give confirmation.

"I'll be fine."

Three words were enough to get Trio outside and give her a false sense of security where the Inccukai was concerned. This fool's hope that somehow, they had become her friend and cared for her more than the paycheck they received from their boss.

When the door squeaked shut, Drag looked at her again. She wanted to see him up close, and wished she'd thought to illuminate the room to take in all of him. He had always possessed his own gravitational field. From the moment she'd been seven, she'd been a sucker for him. The emotional tangle had grown worse as she'd gotten older.

Until that day.

"Better speak fast. Ten minutes."

She anxiously brushed some loose tendrils of red hair behind her ears. "You're always putting time limits on everything. Can we just see how the conversation progresses?"

He took another step toward her. "There's a reason for that. I can only handle you in small doses."

She smiled and let the tension in her frame drain away. This was good territory for her, familiar, this trade of barbs. "That's not what you used to say."

The growl he let loose hit her straight in the damn tits. Her nipples tightened, and she tried to hold onto her anger, not the reality that even now he could still awaken and arouse her body without even touching her. *Fucker.*

"Those words came before you got my arm cut off."

The gap melted away. They were mere inches apart and she wanted to do something insane. *If I rub up against him like a cooncat against a cactus, then yep, I've lost it.* Even if he talked about his arm and her role in him losing the appendage.

"You look better with the cybernetic part."

The gleam in his eye, paired with a half-grin that matched the insanity rolling through her entire body, almost made her jump. She was like a live wire sparking. All she needed to be grounded was a good dose of Drag.

"It squeezes real well, too. Stop fucking around and tell me why you're here. If you say for sex, I'll throw you out right now."

The mention of the word had her standing up straight and taking two steps back. She ran her hands up to the tie holding her red hair back and made sure it was secure. *Idiot.* Top prize for her dumb ass, she'd been ready to kiss, maul and climb him like a goosemert in heat. There were stupid things and then stupider things. Showing that much of her own thoughts to Drag would be bad.

"Here I was hoping if I put some physical pleasure on the line, you might be more willing to help me."

"Afraid my services are already engaged elsewhere. Get to the point."

Jealous heat replaced the tingling sensation on her skin. The question was on the tip of her tongue. She'd demand he tell her the name of the dust honey who he'd decided to be faithful to. *Then I'll rip her fucking throat out.*

A little extreme, and it wasn't like she'd been a saint since Drag had gone to Frog Lick. She'd found her own pleasure with whoever she could. Small pleasures that didn't amount to much but scratched the itch.

"I need your help. A truce for starters. We'll call off the war between us, no more bombs. No retaliation for what happened with Jack. Can you agree to that first?"

Starting out slow would be best. At least her father had always said, *"Don't play all your cards right away."* The old man she'd loved with every ounce of a daughter's admiration had always related his concepts about living to cards and games of chance.

Besides teaching her to play, he had taught her all life's lessons could be seen in the cards. Bridget flipped one out from the hidden pocket of her jacket sleeve. The Ace of Clubs.

"So?"

Drag stroked his jaw. Those strong, callused fingers on his human hand would be rough against her skin. "A truce between Full Throttle and Macintosh. How long before you break it?"

"I get that trust between us doesn't exist. But it's a good word. We truce, then I discuss the business opportunity I have for you."

"We review the opportunity first, then if I like it, we can review terms for your surrender."

She snorted. "I said truce. No way am I surrendering anything."

"You're halfway through your time."

Damn it. He was still holding her to that ten-minute bullshit.

"Fine, we'll just be going in circles anyway." She took a deep breath and summoned the courage to speak the truth amid fear he'd laugh in her face. *Fuck it, I've been laughed at before.* "I need help. My sponsor is planning to overthrow me. He wants me as his wife and won't take no for an answer. He'll put someone else in charge, someone he can control."

Surprisingly, Drag didn't laugh. He stroked his chin and the shadow of growth already covering it. "I take it when you couldn't deliver our engine that proved a problem?"

"More like another excuse he could use against me. My failures just keep racking up. Each one is used to spread discontent among the gang from his plants. Even the bodyguard."

"And what can I do?"

19

This was it—the opening she'd wanted—and now she'd dare to ask him for what he'd denied her twelve years ago.

"You can marry me."

Chapter Two

Twelve years ago

Drag smelled a floral sugar confection, something sweet and heady. The scent wrapped around him, clouding his head and pulling him away from the fabulous dream he'd had and back to reality. The scent developed the barest hint of bitter earth and he opened his eyes.

With a glance down at his bare chest, he caught sight of Bridget's slender fingers and her long nails painted in Macintosh deep green. She was awake. He could tell by the way her breathing was light under the palm of his left hand against her bare back and how she stroked his chest hair.

She leaned up, using her connection with his body to leverage upward. Her lips brushed the shell of his ear as she whispered, "One more day and then I'll tell everyone I'm yours…forever."

Drag couldn't help but smile as he pulled her body flush to his. "I win today and then your father will grant his blessing."

"He'll have no choice. You'll be our top racer and have secured the partnership with our sponsor. My father also promised. We make the perfect pair to lead Macintosh into the future. The end result is obvious." She tugged against his hold and he loosened his grip.

She took the opportunity to straddle him, the thin sheet the only thing separating her naked body from his. Her breasts were glorious, those pale red nipples taut and aching for his mouth. He leaned up to snag one, but Bridget held him at bay with her hands on his shoulders. "Besides, why would my father deny me a chance to have a forever with the only man I'll ever love?"

"Those are strong words." Drag dared to take his eyes off those glorious mounds of flesh to look her in the eyes. A deep green reflected back at him. The color of a lush oasis properly cared for, filled with admiration and desire.

"I wouldn't say them if I didn't mean every syllable." She brought her lips to his, her red hair falling around his face like a curtain blocking the world away.

He reciprocated, melting into her kiss. Allowing himself to drown in sweetness that turned incendiary with a small grind of his hard cock against her core, he silently vowed not to fuck up today. No, he'd have Bridget as his wife, come what may. No amount of sacrificing would be too much to be with her forever.

These were the promises he kept to himself as he moved the sheet away, sank into her and chased off the lingering vestiges of sleep clinging to him.

* * * *

Present day

"I believe I already put myself up for that opportunity," Drag said as he lifted his right arm. "I lost part of my humanity when you decided your words about loving me were bullshit."

The anger in his voice couldn't be disguised. The memories were so firmly ingrained he still had nightmares from that time. A time when he'd been so happy, believing his future was fixed and he'd spend it side-by-side with a woman who held the same ideals as him. A woman who wanted a future like what he was building in Frog Lick. Instead, she'd proven how good of an act she could put on and had betrayed him at the first opportunity.

"Your disgust is understandable."

"Is it, though?" He stepped forward, erasing the last little bit of space between them. Deep down, he was pissed because those forest-green eyes, her red hair and the pale skin dusted with freckles across the bridge of her nose were still making his cock hard.

Twelve years, losing an arm, losing his home, his future… All of it wasn't enough to stop his animal reaction to this woman. She made him want to throw things. Other men would have chosen violence against the object of their frustration, but he'd never raised his hands in anger at a woman, and didn't tolerate such treatment of women or men or, for that matter, anyone.

"I'm not asking for a union in truth. I just need to fake this to cover up what I really want." Her words were coupled with short breaths.

Drag was tempted to touch her, to see if her pulse hammered like his did. Her lips were plump and red, but there were dark circles under her eyes and her cheeks were hollowed out. She hadn't been sleeping well.

Good, she doesn't deserve to.

His internal thoughts were at odds with his human hand. He flexed it at his side, resisting the urge to reach up and cup her cheek. The protective nature he'd always had for her instinctively fluttered to life. *And I need to shut it down.* Instead, he forced himself to focus. "Then what are you after?"

"I need the best to help me break into the Mars Commission office. I know Cheatham is paying off someone, one of the reps. He had to, and if I can get proof, then maybe I can get make sure he doesn't threaten me or Macintosh ever again."

She didn't blink and appeared to be strong in her conviction, but Drag couldn't help but laugh. He laughed so damn hard he took a couple steps back as he wrapped an arm around his stomach. The tell-tale sound of the door to the building creaking open started to calm him.

"Drag...are you okay, brother?" Rune's question made Drag want to tell his brother the whole farce.

I'll do that later.

For now, he needed to end this conversation and get Bridget on her way before that Inccukai sensed any type of threat. Drag got his boisterous chuckle under control and gave a nod. "Yes, I'm fine. Tell the others we'll be done in a few minutes."

The door scraped shut and Rune disappeared from sight. Once he was gone, Drag dared to look at Bridget. Her gaze was green fire, alight. If those eyes possessed any type of physical power, he'd have been dead on the spot.

"I bare my soul and you laugh at me. Why am I not surprised? I thought maybe..." She stomped over to a nearby table and slammed her hands on the top, before shoving at the wooden structure. Her actions produced a rough screech and she let out a frustrated groan. "I take it you won't consider what I said."

He took it as a trap. No other way to look at it. Either Bridget was baiting him in a ploy to get his help and planned to betray him at some moment to make things go her way, or she would ambush them. She had to be angry that none of her other plans had worked.

"Well? Answer me." She shoved at the table again and he had to stop himself from smiling. Her fierce attitude equated to very little physical power. Now she was like an angry cooncat, more bark than bite.

"How do I know this isn't just another attempt to get rid of me and take over Frog Lick yourself? The past two tries didn't work, so you're trying to appeal to me through emotional means."

"If I thought you gave a damn for me anymore, I would've tried something else." She sauntered back toward him, and he couldn't help but watch the sway of her hips…that rocking motion, the easy way she put one foot in front of the other and how each movement reminded him of her naked beneath him. He'd gripped those hips, held them tight as he drove home over and over, just for her to rip that away with her greed and selfishness.

"You might have had better luck that way."

"You're a right bastard. Nuggets of steel you've got."

He grinned. "Afraid those are still human. Only the arm got the full treatment."

Back and forth…this could go on for hours. It would be easy to just slide into bantering with her, keep his anger fresh. He could be a petty bastard sometimes. *With her.*

"What's in this for me again?"

She sighed before propping her hands against her hips. "I said before, didn't I? Cheatham influenced your appeal. The whole reason you're not back to shipbuilding right now is because of him. I've found a way we can get the evidence to prove it. Get him kicked off Mars and out of my life."

Once again, he didn't miss that she wasn't looking at him. No, her gaze was trained on her hands, fingers picking at her nails. Nails she'd bitten down to nothing. They were ragged, different than her usual preference for looking perfectly put together. For half a second he believed her, that Cheatham had driven her to this level of desperation. *She's a damn good actress.*

"If I say I'll consider helping you?"

Her head shot upward, her gaze connecting to his. For a moment he saw the raw emotion there, the Bridget he'd fallen in love with. The same one who'd shed tears when the other kids had been afraid to play with her and Drag had refused to be scared away just because her father was in charge of their gang.

"I'd give you time to consider…though I don't have much of it to spare. You win tomorrow and the window narrows even more."

Drag couldn't help but wink at her. "No guarantees I win. It'll come down to the racer and the driver. Though I wouldn't bet against me."

"You've always been too cocky for your own good."

"And you used to love every minute of it."

Bridget headed for the door first. "I still do."

Drag clenched his fists again, less about anger and more to stop himself from going after her. She licked her lips and paused at the entrance, hands braced, ready to push open the hinged wood separating her from the outside.

"When will you have an answer for me?"

"Find me after the race."

Chapter Three

Twelve years ago

The roars and the boos of the crowd, the sounds of thousands in the stands belting out their frustration or praise as Drag crossed the finish line were music to Bridget's ears. No matter what any individual felt, he'd done it. He'd won the Mars Racing Championship for Macintosh. It was their second win in the history of the races. The last time had been their leader's best friend, long since passed—nearly twenty years since the previous win. This one, though, would secure Macintosh a sponsor, and allow her the chance to marry the man she loved.

"Aah, Bridget. Come here, my girl, and meet Moag Cheatham. You'll be seeing a lot of him with Drag crossing the finish line." Bridget's father, Travis Macintosh, was a bear of a man with a bald head, and a graying, bushy mustache and green eyes that matched hers. Often, he said that he wished she'd been born a man, if only to be able to take over the gang herself. Though with Drag at her side, she'd do just that.

"Coming, Da." She turned away from Drag's victory lap and glanced over at the reedy, graceful gentleman with flowing locks of black hair, wearing a long black coat over a pale blue shirt. He had pale blue eyes as well. They matched his shirt, though his smile didn't quite reach the eyes. "Nice to meet you, Mr. Cheatham."

She extended her hand and he opted to grasp it then yank her up against him. He had more strength than what his visual appearance implied.

"Have all your teeth, do you? A pretty smile, give me one."

His breath was hot and reeked of whiskey. The urge to kick him in the balls warred with her desire to please her father and remain polite. She struggled against his hold, even as her lips broke open and she gave the smile the bastard demanded.

"You're holding me a bit tight."

Cheatham grinned. "And you'll take it rough. Most of you Mars gals do."

Her patience wore thin and she opted to smash her heel onto his foot and ram her knee in his groin. He released her immediately with a shove. "Enjoy your momentary defiance because soon you'll be taught to know your place."

Bridget opened her mouth, then shut it. This was the sponsor her father wanted them to secure. With a quick glance, she noted that her father was distracted as he talked to one of the Mars Racing Commission reps who'd joined them for the last half of the race. There were other sponsors out there and they deserved one that didn't act like their namesake.

A fucking pig. He'll be called crispy if he keeps it up.

"Last time I checked, the only place we need to know is where to put our fists and feet."

Cheatham charged toward her with firm and swift steps. Bridget stood her ground and she plowed her foot right into his balls this time, grinning as he collapsed to the floor. His breath came out in wheezed gasps, her surname repeated on his lips. "Macintosh. Macintosh."

Suddenly arms wrapped around her shoulders and hauled her backward, her father's lackeys pulling her away, judging by the bulging arm muscles and the close-cropped haircuts they wore.

"Colm. Liam. If you both don't let me go—"

"Ignore her and move her away from Cheatham. Bridget, you really need to learn when to be silent and keep your hands to yourself."

Kowtowing to this asshole was what her father would like, but she was Macintosh, and the gang leader's daughter. She'd never bowed down to anyone, ever.

Her father offered a helping hand to Cheatham, between glances of rebuke toward her. "I apologize for her behavior. She's been allowed a bit more freedom than our other women."

Bridget threw her hands up, yanking herself free of Colm and Liam's hold as she did. Then she marched out of the room and into the hallway. Outside of the private viewing area reserved for her family, the clamor of those celebrating or cursing the win increased by tenfold. Macintosh had the glory and her father's would-be sponsor had ruined the moment. She banged a fist against the wall ignoring the looks a few celebrating folks cast her way.

One even had the gall to say, "Why are you upset? Your gang just won."

She growled in return and of course that was the moment her father walked out of the room.

"Da, he put his damn hands on me—"

"And you'll shut your fucking mouth for once, like I said." Her father pointed a single index finger her way, the same one he used to point at any gang member who got lippy with him. But this was one of the rare times he had used it on her. Then he sighed. "That was badly done. Right after the win, too... You couldn't just play the part?"

"I've never played a part in this damn life, and I won't start now. You always said be true to yourself."

Her father sighed and shook his head. "Bridget, everyone has to act a role. It's better to be the one choosing which one you take, instead of having it chosen for you."

For once her father seemed to look his age. Besides the dark tan skin and the lines from being out in the sun too much, his frame looked hunched and his eyes appeared weary.

"Da, I chose. I chose the moment Drag came into my life...so I guess my future was chosen for me. Nothing can change that."

Her father reached for out for her hands, and she settled her palms against his. "Bridget, he's a driver. Not going to amount to much more than winning some trophies and making Mcintosh look good. I entertained the idea when I thought there was nothing better...except I want more than a life for you on this godforsaken planet."

"I don't know how you can say that when I love everything about this place, the rough and sharp edges included. Life isn't without struggle and you always said those who can survive here can do so anywhere." She tried to chase away the grain of anxiety growing steadily in her gut, though it was still there as her father gripped her hands tighter.

"I know you think that's what you want, but it's not. I won't lose you to this place like I lost your mother, so trust in me, please."

"I've always believed in you, Da. My actions should prove as much." The grain was a pile of them now, threatening to buckle her insides. She did her best to hold back the vibrations.

"Good. You can be well-behaved, I know it. Now I need you to take a few breaths, slap on a smile and go back in and apologize to Cheatham. Won't do us to leave today with you insulting your future husband."

* * * *

Present day

Another race—not the championship, but the last regional. This would determine the final spots allowed in the big race. Drag was down there in the Full Throttle racer, driving at speeds Bridget could only dream about. Dreams... She'd had an awful one last night. Reminders of her past and where things had gone wrong the first time, but this time she refused to lose.

With Trio on her right standing guard, she couldn't do much but watch the proceedings. The meeting last night hadn't resolved anything, with Drag telling her to wait until the end of the race. She tapped her foot against the floor. Waiting had never been her style. She liked immediate action. Actions were better than words anyway. *Isn't that how I secured my place as leader of Macintosh?*

Except she'd lost far more in the process. One thing she'd learned over the years was that when a person revealed their true self, there was no going back. Drag wanted her to act the same way her father had, obedient and subservient, the same way all men did. Which was why she'd been surprised to see so many women leading businesses, allowed to say what they wished, controlling their futures in Full Throttle.

It's what we talked about, yet he betrayed me.

In the harsh light of Mars day she'd been second-guessing her decision to ask him for help, but there wasn't anyone else. Not when Cheatham was gathering his own group of supporters. Trio had been sent on plenty of assignments without her input and Bridget gathered they were working on Cheatham's behalf.

The future was too unclear and she needed—

"Ms. Macintosh, I have what you requested."

She glanced away from the track at Colm, one of the few from her father's guard that she believed still stood by her side. "Come in, Colm. Trio, give us a moment."

Cheatham's assassin left the room. Funny how she still didn't know the assassin's true name—additional proof she couldn't trust those beside her. Colm stood next to the seat now vacated. He was not as much of a hulking figure as he'd been in her youth and his light brown beard was now intertwined with gray.

"Here, what you asked for." He shoved an envelope toward her and she accepted the faded brown paper.

"Did anyone see you?"

"No, I retrieved it from the hiding place you'd mentioned. Didn't even see the person who put it there."

Bridget opened the envelope, anxious to pull out the information within, when she stopped herself short with Colm standing over her. "You can go now. Please stand outside the door and do not let anyone enter until I say."

"Yes'm."

Colm's departure was quiet, yet quick. A roar let loose from the attendees surrounding the track as the leader boards was updated with the final results. Drag had indeed won, and while a Bridget from twelve years ago remembered the elation she had felt then, it was good to recall how short-lived such excitement could be. How all too easily, joy could turn to terror, then anger and retribution.

She ripped open the envelope and removed the paper. Here was what she needed to secure Drag's help, the proof that Cheatham had interfered with Full Throttle's appeal. Opening the paper, she read through the transcript.

The trade better have been worth it.

Bridget folded the paper and tucked it into the shape support she wore to secure her breasts. No one would suspect or bother to search there. Not if they wanted to keep their arms. She pressed a button and the door opened.

"Yes'm."

"I'm ready to go. Escort me to the pits. I need to meet with the Full Throttle leader." She stood and walked to the door, trying to gather her strength and calm. This day was so reminiscent of the past, the memories like beautiful fruits spoiled by invading worms. She'd never escaped her father's actions and in return her reactions to the news that she would marry Cheatham.

She vowed to never let a man tell her what she would or wouldn't do. Even Drag... In the end, if he didn't help, she'd find another way.

As she walked out of her dedicated viewing box, Colm flanked one side of her and Trio took position on the other. They walked through a growing throng of people, heading down ramps to the main level. The conversations boomed around her with the excitement of Full Throttle qualifying not once, but twice with two different drivers. The rumors of the racer, along with the use of NiteOx, spilled from people's lips.

No surprise there, as Bridget knew damn well Full Throttle had designed an engine that could handle NiteOx legally. The substance was deemed too dangerous to be mixed with marsanium sludge fuel. There were plenty of people who'd lost their lives in those experiments. From the moment she'd learned of Drag's triumph in the mechanics bay and with the Mars Racing Commission, she'd tried to thwart them. First by destroying a racer and almost their driver, Hemi, then by trying to steal the designs to the engine. Finally she'd gone a little mad.

Dumb to try and start a turf war.

Though she'd acted to show Cheatham she could be ruthless. Her people were divided on warring or not. They all wanted a win. They wanted fame and glory that brought the showers of gold leaf and supplies they couldn't get on Mars. The members of Macintosh, like her, had become complacent, believing they would keep their sponsor by producing quality ore and some good ships. But Cheatham wanted racing success — and he wanted Bridget to fail.

"Are you sure about this?" Trio asked as the three of them came to a stop in front of a door that would take them away from the public and underground toward the pits where drivers and their crews worked on cars.

"I'm going to get an answer to my proposal, that's all. If he turns me down, then I'll know where I stand."

Trio didn't know the details of the proposal, only that she hadn't received a response. She kept her back straight, her walk steady even as she clenched her fists and asked herself for the dozenth time... *Why are you trying to bargain with him? He already betrayed you once.*

The same question had come up from the first moment she had considered appealing to Drag for help, but it came down to one thing. When Drag gave his word, he stuck by it, with the exception of never leaving her side, though those circumstances had been strenuous. She'd chased her damn mind into a frenzy with those thoughts.

Drag was consistent. He tended to fight for the oppressed and damn it, while she hated admitting it, the Macintosh gang had been put into a box and held hostage by a tyrant. No matter how much she tried to initiate her goals, she was thwarted from enacting true change.

They cleared the racetrack, and she heard voices ahead as the tunnel widened. There were hoots and cheers, along with the smell of champagne, sickly sweet, being poured everywhere. Disgusting, wasteful habit. Though better than drinking the shit.

"You two hang back a bit behind me. I don't want to appear a threat," she said as she approached the opening to the Full Throttle area.

She caught a glimpse of Drag, smiling. Dust and slithers, he had a beautiful smile. It was bright and made him seem younger. She missed how he'd looked at her with such a wide grin back in the old days and wondered who the hell he was gracing such beauty with now.

But her ability to find out was cut short as Drag's dark doppelganger blocked her path, stopping her from moving into the bay.

"Well, well...figures my best friend wins a race and you show up. Heard you were poking around Frog

Lick last night, too." Snapper's words dripped with derision.

Bridget dared to look up. Snapper had the upper hand over her, even in the two-inch heeled boots she wore. Her half-brother's eyes were filled with the same scorn and hatred as his voice. If only he'd understood he'd been a threat to her claim as gang leader.

"I have business with Drag, that's it. Don't need to pull your guard dog routine."

Snapper held up his cybernetic arm and flexed, clenching his fist tight. "It's not for show. You try to mess with him, and I'll bite back this time."

He had every right to hate her, and back then she'd gotten a little stupid when she'd found out her father's plans. She'd turned desperate in her bid to win back the future she'd wanted. Since then, well... *I'm still learning my lessons.*

Bridget smirked as she cocked her head to the side. "I've got protection too. And trust me, they're a lot faster than you. At least I think they are, but I'm always willing to place bets and see."

"Name the fucking time and place," Snapper said as he puffed up his chest and took a step toward her, invading what little space she had. "When I'm done with that piece of shit, I just might go back on my promise to never hit a woman."

"She's no woman." The male voice behind Snapper was one she vaguely recognized. Then Snapper was shoved back.

"Hold up, not here." Drag had interfered.

The hell?

Bridget was prepared for this to go sour, but she had to school her features fast to overcome the momentary jaw drop at Drag pushing Snapper away from her. It hadn't been for her sake—that was for sure. *I need to remember that.*

Snapper frowned, the grimace on his face enhancing the small indentions above his eyes. Just like their father's. "Fine, but it's your funeral even talking to her. Let's go, and leave these two to chat."

There were others in the room with them. Ones she hadn't paid attention to until now. Hemi, the half cybernetic driver, who was now married to the Aurestral leader. Nor did she fail to see the one who'd accused her of not being a woman…Jack. She'd taken a finger from him. Every single male standing in the room had been marked by her and a part of her deep inside wanted to apologize…but then again, when had any man apologized to her?

Never, fucking never.

"I believe congratulations are in order then?" She found her words easily enough as the very men eyeballing her with malcontent walked by. "Of course, impressive you got something done where the rest of them couldn't."

"This fucking bitch," Jack muttered as he passed.

"Yes. Yes, I am…but I'm not afraid to own it." She would, too. To everlasting loneliness, she'd never let anyone get the best of her.

"Enough!" Drag yelled and the others marched out a bit faster.

Once the area had cleared he spoke again. "Get rid of the bodyguards or we're not talking."

The low commanding bass of his voice sent a shiver up her spine. She had always loved when he took control. She'd had to be on all the time and he'd give her something… *Fuck.*

"Colm, take Trio and go get a drink or something. I'll meet you at the tunnel entrance in a half an hour."

She half expected pushback, but instead the two walked off. For once things were going her way.

When their footsteps got smaller, he looked at her and she stared back, wishing he'd smile again.

"You had to come in here and cause a scene."

She grinned. "No other way for me to enter a room and you know it."

"You still don't care, do you?"

She cared too much—that had always been the problem. But she couldn't let them see it. Never. A woman didn't let anyone observe how they might beat her. Not if she wanted to win in the long run.

"I care about one thing—"

"Yourself."

She winked at him. "You know it."

Reaching into her shirt for the paper tucked in her bodice, she didn't miss Drag's gaze following and lingering on the hint of breast she was showing off. Did he recall the color of her nipples? They were hard now as she considered he might. The edge of the paper cut her finger as she prolonged the motion to keep his gaze on her.

"Take it out already," he said with a snap of his fingers.

"Damn, you could kill a woman's libido, you know?" She whisked the paper out, hissing as it pressed against the cut, leaving a drop of blood behind on the paper. "This information came at a hefty price. I just cut myself."

He snatched the paper from her grip. "You deserved it after nearly causing a riot down here. Why couldn't you wait another half hour until they cleared out?"

"I don't have the patience for that. You said you wanted proof. Right, well, the paper is proof. Cheatham got your appeal to the Mars Shipping

Commission revoked. He won't stop there. All of Wespero would benefit from him being gone."

Drag looked over the paper, the transcript of the conversation during the commission session. He read aloud, "This commission hereby reads and submits testimony from the Macintosh sponsor, Moag Cheatham, who states that Frog Lick and the Full Throttle gang are still rebuilding after the arrest of their previous leader and would potentially spread bad representation by building subpar products due to lack of sufficient mechanics… Are you fucking kidding me?"

"He's not." She sucked the blood from her paper cut. The bitter iron on her tongue was a reminder that this wound was nothing compared to what she'd suffer if he didn't agree. "Are you mad enough to help me now?"

Drag crumbled the paper with his cybernetic hand and kept working it, over and over with increasingly fast movements until dust started to sprinkle out of his clenched metal fist and onto the floor. "I can't make a decision today, Bridget. I don't run my gang like you or your father did. I need inputs from others because it won't be just me engaging. It would be everyone. Your little stunt today doesn't help."

She stood ramrod straight and narrowed her gaze. "I'm not putting on a fake front for anyone, ever again. What you see right here is what you get."

What space between them melted away and Bridget's inhale faltered a bit as she got a gaze into the clear blue of Drag's eyes. He could always get her lost in them.

"Honey, you've been hiding behind a façade since the day I met you. The funny part is you were always your best self when you stopped acting."

Chapter Four

Twelve years ago

"We fucking did it!" Snapper wrapped Drag up in a bear hug just as he cleared his first leg out of the racer. "We're champions."

Then the liquor spraying started. People shook up bottles of ale or anything fizzy they could get their hands on...like sticky sweet champagne. Hell, he'd have to snag one of those to have with Bridget tonight, when they celebrated in private.

Though after today, they might not have to hide things. He'd ask their gang leader for her hand, to officially be bonded, married to her and supporting her as the next in line to take over Macintosh. He found the focus to squeeze Snapper in return and slap his best friend on the back.

"Let me go, so I can get a drink and wash up. I smell like track and sludge fuel."

"Damn straight, a better smell there never was because it's paired with victory!" Snapper shouted as he released Drag, who landed on the floor and took a few steps to steady himself.

Snapper then moved on, going to the other mechanics in the bay and the helpers with more embraces. The grins, the laughter, the joy... Drag was more than happy to be the cause of it. The adrenaline that had pumped hot and heavy through his veins during the race was fading fast. Though the celebration around him buoyed his flagging energy, there was someone notably not in the pit with them.

"Where's Bridget?" he asked as his brother Rune came up and wrapped him in a hug.

"She hasn't come down yet, but I'm sure they're surrounded up there. You heard the cheers. Over half in attendance were excited about the win."

Those words buoyed his mood even higher. He hadn't just delivered for the gang, but for the entirety of Wespero. He turned to helping Snapper pack up the racer, all the while making jokes and enjoying the mood around him. Drag vowed he'd catch up with Bridget later back in Macintosh.

"Quit looking for her," Snapper said as they drove into town. A crowd lined both sides of the main road past the town sign. A smaller group took the racer to the mechanics bay, but Snapper and Drag drove their hauler toward the bonfire already lit near the leader's house. This was where they gathered to celebrate big moments for Macintosh, not in a bar or closed space, but out in the open. One of the ways Macintosh prided themselves on being different.

"Parties are meant to be heard for miles." Bridget's dad, Travis had said that many times over the years when planning for a big event.

Several tables were on the far side of the fire circle with trays of bread, fire-grilled meat, cheese wheels and crates of fruits provided by their soon-to-be sponsor. A big cask of brew had already been opened and people dipped giant mugs in to fill them without restraint.

They were going all out tonight, more so than they typically dared because Drag's win would mean a sponsor. Sponsors meant flash for the gang to buy food, medical supplies and much-needed items they couldn't always get from trades or the land itself. This would secure the gang's future and his place beside Bridget.

Bridget, whom he still hadn't seen hours after the race. Even among the crowd gathering in celebration around the already roaring bonfire, she wasn't there. He decided he couldn't wait for her to confirm anything. He'd waited plenty and now it was time Travis heard him out.

No, I'll speak to him now.

He replayed the words in his head as he climbed the dozen steps to the house's main entrance. The leader's home had been put on up on ballasts made of red brick, formed from the clay. Other homes were similar, but they didn't sit as high as Travis Macintosh's — a symbol of how he watched over them all, took care of their needs.

Pausing before the door, a thick tapestry of triple-layered cloth, woven with the Macintosh gang symbol, hung by rungs that rested on a thick wooden rod, Drag knew what he had to say, but feared he hadn't done enough. *No, I won't doubt.*

Bridget had told him this was the way to get her father to agree to grant Drag her hand. He trusted her with his very life. If she said winning the race would be enough, then he believed her.

Taking a deep breath, Drag pulled back the entry cover and stepped instead. "Macintosh leader," he called out.

The light was low, just a couple lit lanterns in the corners of the main room that boasted a couch and floor pillows. Again, the leader preferred his guest sit on the floor and he above them. Out of deference to his hard work, and because his body was old.

The clatter of objects falling to the floor brought his attention to the leader's private room. Where Bridget's room was to the right of the main entrance, the leader's was to the left. Drag moved forward at a quick clip, fearful of Travis having health trouble. It was true that Travis Macintosh had once been a strong and great man, one who'd sacrificed many things, including his wife, in the process of creating the greatness of Macintosh. But he was old, in a way frail, and not as fast as he'd been.

Bridget had lamented her fears that her father would pass without a proper heir in place. Not to mention her ongoing frustration and worry Macintosh wouldn't accept a female as their leader. There was a big emphasis on a woman's place within the gang. They didn't hold jobs, were forbidden from schooling and took care of the men who worked to provide a better future for all.

They would change all that antiquated thinking. With Drag as her husband, Bridget could make the argument to rule with an equal partner, and he would let her take charge. They would change this gang into a place where everyone, no matter their gender, could thrive.

He crossed the room, pausing every couple steps, listening for additional noises. Nothing stuck out at first, but as he got closer to the leader's room, a raspy voice was mumbling. He couldn't make out the words as he reached for the heavy covering that hung over the doorway. When he lifted it up, the glimmer of metal flashed, reflecting light. In Bridget's hand was the knife, coated in blood, and her father lay on his bed in a pool of blood.

"Bridget, what have you done?"

* * * *

Present day

"She interrupted our celebration for this shit?" Snapper leaned back in his chair, arms crossed and scowling at the 'proof' Bridget had handed Drag hours before.

Drag and his closest confidants were locked up in the backroom of the Watering Hole while everyone else danced and drank the evening away. Some of this group had been with him from the beginning when he'd been forced to leave his home gang and find somewhere new.

Snapper was included, along with Drag's brother Rune, and Rune's wife Petal. Over the years, they had added Jack, their brother in the cybernetic trials that had repaired their missing limbs. There were others, but for this evening Drag had assembled those who would be impacted the most by the next steps he took.

Fuck, the whole gang might suffer.

"It's a pretty big deal. This means that bastard has been working against us since the moment Drag took over as leader of Frog Lick," Rune added as he picked up the paper to read it again.

"What does any of this matter? We win the championship, we can get our own sponsor, have someone willing to back us." Jack's point was valid, too.

"It matters because Cheatham could spread more lies and stop sponsors from expressing interest," Rune replied.

They were silent for a moment before Snapper sat up straight and clicked his teeth. "Getting into any deal with her is asking for more trouble and you fucking know it."

"You don't care at all?" Drag hated those words coming out of his mouth, but he couldn't help it. Once he'd made a promise... That was what a gang tattoo meant. Then he'd run away, leaving behind so many. He'd escaped with Rune, Petal and Snapper. A few had defected later and joined up with Full Throttle after he'd taken over, but there were so many who he'd abandoned.

"Macintosh chose when they didn't believe us the first time. We warned them all, cried out for backing and support. Instead, she took my arm, then made you fight and took yours. Bridget's power mad. This play is because she fears losing what little she stole. If you can't see that—"

"And why not take the risk? If we win, we could get leverage over a powerful enemy," Gaia said from the doorway. She stood there, her pale blonde braids swinging past her hips as she sauntered into the room carrying a tray of mugs and bowls.

"Who said we needed your opinion?" Jack asked.

The bartender sidled up next to Jack and plonked him on the head with the underside of her tray. "Drag said when he took over, everyone in this town had a say in how their gang was run. This decision involves all of us, but there's too much animosity to get consensus."

Gaia was correct. If Drag had felt more confident about involving others in this decision and believed he could get a decent answer, he would have held a vote session. But this situation was too volatile and had the potential to spread their rumored turf war with Macintosh into a territory-wide issue.

"Gaia is right, and that's the only reason we aren't addressing the whole group out in the main room now. I brought you here to give me your opinions, and Snapper... I know yours. What about you, Rune?"

His younger brother, a miniature version of him in almost every way, except Rune had both arms, ran a hand through his sun-kissed blonde hair. The man spent most of his days outdoors working the airponics setup and the hydroponics plants. He was the reason Frog Lick had survived from the moment they'd lost the ability to build ships.

"Brother, I don't want to see you hurt, but I have to agree with Gaia that taking no action might put us in a worse place. We need to secure our future and Cheatham is a direct threat to it." His brother made a fair point, yet again, though Drag was well aware that Rune would back whatever decision he opted for, no questions asked.

"Isn't Bridget the lessor of two evils?" Jack asked. "I mean, sure she took my finger, but in reality, we beat her. We could beat her again. This Cheatham guy has other resources."

"And he brought in the Inccukai." Drag couldn't let them forget that part, the momentary fear he'd seen in Bridget's eyes. This needed to be about Full Throttle's future, not hers, and he needed to remember the knife…what he'd lost to her after finding her standing over her father's dead body.

He flexed his cybernetic fist. The movement sent a rush of nanites coursing through his system, like a temporary high. It reminded him of the strength he now possessed.

She brought us here.

"That scary bastard with the creepy eyes and all those cloth coverings?" Snapper shook his head. "Gina said the damn thing reminds her of something she read in old Earth files about a mummy. A creature wrapped up in cloth strips that can drain the life from people."

"Did you know the damn thing has a name?"

Jack chuckled. "Oh yeah, that's a good depiction of them. Can't tell what they are besides deadly and damn intimidating."

"What's its name?" Rune asked at the same time.

"Trio," Drag replied.

"Allying with Bridget helps us get to know our enemy." Gaia had long since set the mugs and bowls down on the table and now stood with her empty tray tucked against her hip. "Besides, nothing to say you couldn't prepare to double-cross her, if necessary."

Drag moved to pick up a mug and took a long swallow. The cool taste of water washed down his throat. He should have been drinking in celebration. Instead he was trying to keep his head for the business at hand. "Tell me more."

"Easy enough. You go along with her plan and work with Gina to come up with some alternate options. Her brain is the best at this. She could finesse all the possibilities. Put us on the winning path." Gaia started to move toward the door. "Think on it and remember — there's a whole gang out there believing happy thoughts, so the winning team better make an appearance before they start to doubt things."

The idea wasn't bad.

Jack added his agreement, along with Rune. Snapper was the only hold-out.

His best friend picked up a mug of ale and pounded it back, then he slammed the empty on the table before grabbing another. "It's not bad as far as plans go. My Gina always has contingencies for her contingencies, so I'm not worried there. What I'm concerned about is you."

Snapper pointed a finger straight at Drag. He could've guessed this was where Snapper's focus would be. He'd never admit it to anyone in this room, but Snapper was right. The man had been by his side from the first moment Drag had fallen for Bridget, from the years spent watching him go from friends chasing each other in dusty roads to first kisses, then lovers determined to be together forever.

Snapper had seen Drag get his heart broken, dreams smashed, and they'd both lost part of their bodies in the aftermath. They'd spent plenty of time tossing back blame and accusations, but the one thing Snapper had never forgotten was how far gone Drag had been for Bridget.

"What's the concern?" he asked.

His question had everyone silent like the moment before a race started. Even Gaia froze with her hand on the door handle.

Snapper nodded. "All right, can you keep your shit together and not get caught up in Bridget's games? She'll lead you right back into a damn collar and sacrifice you without a second thought to get what she wants."

There was the blatant truth just thrust at him like a knife to the gut. He'd considered the same, too. She wanted him to propose, to fake an engagement and alliance between their groups. Something like that would rile everyone up and those things played back to the dreams he'd once held so dear to his heart. But his endgame wasn't a happily ever after—it was survival for Full Throttle, any way he could get it.

"Yeah, just leave it to me."

* * * *

The whistle echoed amid all the dead racers and ship guts of the junkyard. A short whistle, followed by two long ones. Bridget had arrived. Drag took his time navigating through the piles of a mechanic's dream as he moved in the direction of continued signal.

He rounded a giant pile of wiring to find her propped against the frame of an old racer that had caught fire, if the crispy gray and black colors mixed with rust were any indication.

Bridget had her hair up, wrapped in a bun. Sun goggles perched on her head and she wore a long rust-colored trench jacket over matching pants and some leather-hide boots. She was gorgeous as always. There was no point in denying it to himself since his dick was already twitching at a mere glance.

Probably because he could recall her naked form, and even now wondered if it looked the same. *I need to get laid.*

Hell, he'd been saying that every moment he'd had to interact with Bridget and still couldn't bring himself to find some no-strings companionship. Gaia had turned him down again, though in years past she'd been perfect for a romp. That would have made this easier, but then it would ruin the façade he was considering. *Exactly why Gaia told me to get lost.*

He took another glance, watching as Bridget whistled for him, pursing her lips together, almost as if in a kiss. *Fuck.* Snapper had a right to be worried if Drag's first thoughts seeing this woman always swayed toward his cock. *Time to stop screwing around.*

When he stepped out into view, the whistle she'd started to let loose died a slow strangled death. He kept his steps measured, refusing to let her think her reaction to him affected his body or mind in any way, though he took note of her perusal, how her gaze traveled the length of him not once, not twice, but three times. On the last one, she lingered on his exposed cybernetic arm. He wore a hefty leather vest over his sleeveless shirt. The Full Throttle flag was inked on his left biceps. The Macintosh symbol had long been lost when his right arm had been cut off. Maybe she recalled where it had once rested, how that part of his connection to her would never return.

She ensured that particular outcome.

She spoke first. "I was starting to think you were going to stand me up."

"I thought about it a couple of times, but ultimately couldn't."

She grinned, though once more the smile never reached her eyes. Not like the ones he used to be able to coax from her. "Because I'm irresistible?"

"No. Full Throttle voted to go this path and I prefer the idea of not being in a turf war and losing my people to senseless violence."

Her lips were now on a downturn, and she stood straight, summoning her full height with the help of those boots she wore. "People die every day."

"True, but what we were headed toward would mean deaths for those who don't deserve the trip yet."

"This alliance could end the same way."

That flash of defiance, her refusal to kowtow to anything. She was as fierce as a damn slither...and hell if he didn't admire her for the bravado.

"It could, but know that I'll be taking steps to ensure it doesn't."

"Wouldn't expect anything less. So, will you marry me?"

Drag shook his head. "No. But I'll play the role of a man courting you, and an alliance in the hopes of marriage."

"Isn't that the same thing?" Bridget now had her hands on her hips, echoing similar frustration to his own. She threw around the offer of marriage without care.

"No, we're going to mimic a couple coming close to the prospect, but I'm not crossing that line. Today, tomorrow or in a million solar years. You lost the chance to marry me in any capacity..." He let the words die off, because why say more about what had happened. He couldn't trust her to explain herself. She had refused to then, so why would she now?

"When I had them cut your arm off. I know."

The urge to ask her again, to beg her to tell him why, rose up like fresh bile in his throat, ready to burst forth and burn all of him coming out. He swallowed hard and kept his mouth shut for a moment.

She broke the silence first. "So, sun's dropping, it's about to get cold and I'd like to head back before the Inccukai comes looking for me. Let's get this going."

"How did you sneak away in the first place?"

"I had them take care of some other business for me, collections. Trio does a good job and Cheatham prefers when someone he trusts handles his flash. I have another solar hour left before I'll be missed."

That was the biggest challenge with all this – she manipulated others for the sake of her own purposes. What did someone need to offer her in order to renege on his agreement to help?

"Before you tell me your big plan, care if we set some ground rules?"

She eyed him with a bit of suspicion, but gave a shrug. "Sure."

"First up, no more lying to me. I get the truth, unvarnished and ugly. I don't mind having to work in dangerous situations, but I can't be successful without honesty. A least between us. If you want to lie to everyone else, go right ahead."

Bridget stamped her foot on the ground and crossed her arms before muttering a begrudging, "Fine."

"Second, I get the opportunity to alter any of these plans if I find a better option when we get to the moment of execution. I'll make sure that you're not negatively impacted by those decisions. And, three" – this would be the one hardest to voice – "you don't touch me, in any way, unless you let me know beforehand and I agree to it."

She scoffed. "No one will believe we're in love if that's the case."

"Hey, tell them I suffer PTSD, that I can't bear to be touched without warning. But that's the way this has to be, no debate, or I'm out."

"Whatever… Then I'll warn you. But you want the truth, I think you're acting like a goosemert's bum. Backing me into a corner with no option but to accept your terms."

It was Drag's turn to smile. "Seems fair, since you did the same to me twelve years ago."

Twelve years…and fuck if he wasn't still a little hung up on this woman who'd gotten away from him. He hadn't been lying to Snapper when he'd told him over a year ago that he never regretted loving Bridget. He couldn't, and he wanted to find love again someday.

Just not with her…though she still set fire to his very skin. Every nerve of his body lit up in an excitement he didn't even find behind the wheel of a racer anymore. Sparring with her was something out of his memory and he didn't want to lose this blast to the past.

"Enough. I agree to all of it." Bridget leaned back head looking to the darkening sky. "Now we talk about the plan. We need proof. Audio, holo-video or picture evidence of Cheatham interfering in your case or threatening other members of the commission. Without something physical, it will be hard to turn the commission against him. So, we plant recording devices in the championship dome. Cheatham has assured me he'll be here for the race and that Macintosh will compete."

Fucking laughable. "He's full of shit. I won the last spot for Wespero, secured it. The top two from each territory go on, with a third honorable mention. Macintosh barely made top four."

"If you get disqualified, we would be in...but the bottom line is we need to spy on the commission, on their meetings with sponsors, leaders for those partaking in the championship race and any other areas as well. Once we secure proof, we present it to other leaders in Wespero, Aurestral and Aurora. We get enough of them outraged and on our side, we could force the racing commission to take action."

Drag found her proposal interesting, but—"You're relying too much on the hope that the commission will care about the corruption. You and I both know that many of those who've served have grown to enjoy their positions and comforts. Strip those away and they will react the way caged animals do and lash out."

He'd watched his own cries for assistance fall on deaf ears. The Mars Shipping and Racing Commissions didn't want to hear about the coup within Macintosh, about the suffering of Frog Lick. Those were matters the leaders should have considered when making choices. They were gang-related issues, not things the commission deigned to interfere with, though they wanted to institute all these rules to curb free thought and drive consistency that would line their pockets.

"Well, we cross that slither hole when we come to it. The more pressing matter is first convincing both our gangs that we're no longer enemies." Bridget had relaxed her stance a bit, but at the mention of their gangs, she was back to wringing her gloved hands. "How do you plan to do that?"

"I'll show you."

Chapter Five

Bridget clasped a hand over her belly, trying to will away the clenching muscles within. She'd been this way since Drag had stomped off in the junkyard and left her alone. Then she'd ventured back to her home in Macintosh, alone and full of nerves. He'd said he would show her how he'd make those in their gangs believe in their alliance, but she feared what such a display might bring.

She couldn't risk bloodshed right now even if she'd pretended not to care with Drag. There was already plenty of animosity brewing from the Macintosh group, pissed that Full Throttle had won the race, even after she'd encouraged her people to sabotage their racer the first time.

Deep down, Bridget regretted almost killing that driver. She hadn't intended for the explosion to be that big. No, it was supposed to go off when the racer got over sixty miles per hour and instead it went when the situation reversed as the racer slowed down at the end.

Like every other decision that had blown up in her face the past twelve years, she had no choice but to embrace what occurred. Let her people celebrate her resolve to stick it to their Wespero rivals led by the betrayer, Drag—the one who led Macintosh to victory, but abandoned the gang when he wouldn't be allowed to rule.

The lie she'd clung to, the story Cheatham had spread for her... It had benefited him and her in that moment. She had refused to marry anyone, not when her people needed a leader. When Drag had killed her father.

Lies. Too many of them. I just want to make things right for once.

It seemed no matter what approach she took, things unraveled and not in her favor. Cheatham's latest threat meant her time as the Macintosh leader was about to end and there would be no way to fight him, not when he had placed an assassin and how many other spies within her ranks. If her years as the leader had proven anything, there were too many people that could be bought. There was no true loyalty in running things the way her father had.

Drag is right.

She hated him in that moment, jealous of how all his gang members looked up to him. His charisma, good looks and eager promises... Would they sway some of her people as well? Her stomach clenched anew. She grabbed a glass and filled it with recycle. A drink might help her clear her head, but nothing strong. A clear mind and focus would be needed if Drag showed up in Macintosh territory today.

Her slow, steady swallow was interrupted by a teenage messenger who burst into the room. "Leader, there were arrivals spotted on the edge of town. The haulers are bearing the Full Throttle symbol."

She spit out some of the water, sputtering on what little had tried to enter her airways. A couple coughs later, she managed to croak, "Where's Trio?"

"Still dealing with this month's disbursement."

"Tell the others to let them enter, no violence. I'll hear them out here in the main square and meet them at the steps."

"But Leader—"

"Do as instructed or you'll be without food for a week!"

The boy, his brown eyebrows furrowed in confusion, turned and ran out of the room. There were other things she could have yelled about, like his presence in her private quarters without knocking. Her father would've expressed outrage that enemies were allowed to pass their borders without being stopped first.

The sticklers will be whispering about that.

She stood and grabbed for her vest, for a pair of guns that would rest in the side holsters. Her stomach was in complete riot, at odds with the hard gaze she forced herself to hold in the mirror reflection.

"No one makes you do what you don't want to. No one makes you less than. You are Bridget fucking Macintosh." She announced those words to her reflection as she did every morning before she left her room.

Pulling her hair back in a ponytail, she gave herself one more glance. There were the little differences—the freckles along the bridge of her nose and cheeks were more prominent, the small lines at the edges of her eyes longer and the scar trailing down the side of her temple was faded, but the memory of how it had gotten there hadn't.

She prayed to whatever deity existed that today would go in her favor instead of the opposite. That maybe for once she'd placed her bets on the right person, the right opportunity.

Walking out of her room, she dared to look across the living space to the entrance to her father's room, the one she refused to enter or occupy after that fateful night. "I had no choice. You gave me no option, and then still took everything away from me."

No matter how many times she had tried to speak to him, silently or out loud, she could never hear his response in her head. His voice was a long-distant memory and the guilt that she should have felt was replaced with anger.

She shook her head, clearing the frustration away, clenching her fists and swiping at her eyes, at the tears trying to gather. Usually, she did so well avoiding this type of reaction, but today with Full Throttle at her gates and another confrontation with the man she'd once expected to spend forever with, her walls were weak and being breached by everything from her past.

No time for this today.

Stomping a single booted foot on the floor twice, she willed her body's shaking, the teeter-totter emotions, to subside. A knock at her outer doorframe announced the return of the messenger. "Leader, they are almost to the center. The rest of the gang is assembling."

"Coming."

She took a deep breath and stepped outside. The sun was midway in the sky, and she pulled her sun goggles down to protect her vision. She didn't want anyone getting a glimpse at her reaction to the hauler circling around the giant fire pit that made up the center of Macintosh, Drag in the front seat, his friend Jack driving.

One other hauler brought a few others — no one she recognized, but witnesses to whatever occurred here today. *This is a statement.*

Her stomach cramps were replaced with butterflies as Drag hopped out of the hauler before it even came to a stop and started marching up the small flight of twelve steps toward her. He'd been impressive twelve years ago, but in that sleeveless hooded shirt, with the gleam of his cybernetic arm shining in the sunlight, he was more intimidating now.

"You're here." The words emerged from her mouth a bit breathless, instead of like a statement.

He lifted his head, blue eyes meeting her gaze and grinned. "As promised."

"How do we do this?" She had already caught the scowls on her gang's faces. The way the women were shielding their children. The men were fists and weapons at the ready. A single spark of her displeasure would start the fight. The people wanted retribution, craved revenge. Full Throttle had blown up their water-processing warehouse. A couple years of work had been ruined the last time Full Throttle had visited Macintosh.

"I said leave that to me," he replied with wink. Then he turned and faced their audience.

Bridget caught sight of Trio on the edge of the crowd working their way through the group. She crossed her fingers behind her back.

Please don't let them try to kill him.

"People of Macintosh, I know you remember me as I remember most of you. I'm here today to begin the process of making amends. To Macintosh." Drag motioned in her direction. "To your leader, and of course to start our path toward alliance. In truth, to court your leader and show Bridget I'm not the man who once left you, power-hungry and mad, but one who is ready to be a path to Macintosh's future."

Her heart thudded in her chest. The proclamation was so unlike the one he'd made on these very steps years ago, the one where he'd accused her of being a killer and demanded she confess.

"Prove it!" one of her mechanics yelled.

A ship builder followed. "Yeah, fight!"

"Fight! Fight! Fight!"

The single word grew to a deafening roar as her people demanded he prove his commitment through physical combat. If he won, then they'd believe him. Losing meant he was a liar. It was a weird philosophy and one she hadn't agreed with from a young age, but it was as close to a form of worship as her people got. When disagreements broke out, the settling of such was battle, whether women, men or children. Hell, she'd seen eyes lost, lives ended and more over something as simple as a woman accusing another of wanting to sleep with her man.

"I figured they'd go this route. Twelve years and this place hasn't changed a bit." Drag still smiled, but there was a sadness in his eyes.

"Hard to break what they've believed in for so long." She left out the part where they had been supposed to change things together.

"Then there's no choice, I guess." He faced the crowd once more, arms upraised. "Good people of Macintosh, if it's a fight you demand to prove my commitment, then choose your representative!"

The crowd roared and Bridget was swept away by the familiarity and the fear that she'd lose him a second time.

* * * *

Twelve years ago

Drag… He'd seen her.

She opened her mouth, but no words came out. Then he was gone, running away from her. Cheatham's voice, filled with a dreadful calm, echoed in her ears. "Was that the man you'd planned on ruling with?"

Shit. Shit. Shit!

The knife clattered out of her hand to the floor, narrowly avoiding her feet. She needed to get a hold of herself. Cheatham had made her a deal, and now it might be ruined.

"That was him." She took a step back, avoiding looking at her father, her eyes on the man who offered a chance at the future she wanted if she took her father out of the picture.

"You know that he'll have to be dealt with, unless you think he can keep quiet." Cheatham was deadly calm, his words matter-of-fact.

She'd expected to have time, to go to him without her father's blood staining her clothes and tell him the sacrifice she'd had to make, for him, for their future. Instead, he'd run at the first glimpse of her, though this wasn't a view that left the best impression. "He'll keep silent. I know he'll listen to me."

"I'll have my men pick him up and hold him until you've finished the other part."

Drag would doubt her even more if Cheatham's men held him. How would he listen to her then? She needed more time.

"Bridget...do we still have a deal?"

"Hmm?" She needed to go to her lover and tell him how her father was going to betray them both. He'd promised her to Cheatham, and worse, had refused to let them lead the gang.

"The bastard son. You said there would be one more threat. The agreement to let you take over is based on you ensuring there are no disputes for the role as leader. No other children are going to appear and lay a claim."

She leaned down and picked up the knife, wiping the blood off on her father's blankets. "There won't be. I'll take care it."

As she walked out of the door, into the party, moving within the dark between partygoers celebrating the Macintosh win, she felt less like herself than ever before, limbs heavy, her body sluggish but moving forward on autopilot, as if she was just a bystander watching from afar as her physical form operated on its own.

Drag had to trust in her, even if her next steps might seem extreme. The hold Cheatham had over Macintosh's future meant she had no choice. They would be in charge. She just had to remember that was what all this sacrificing was for.

She was able to steer clear of the brightest parts of the group mingling between casks of ale, tables of food and the bonfire. There was music echoing around her but her gaze stayed focused on the small house in the distance, the one that was next to the mechanics bay.

It had been a gift to Snapper, her father's favorite mechanic. In an off-hand conversation with one of his closest confidants, she'd heard the truth…her half-brother, born to another woman, before her father took her mother as his official wife. Snapper was the mistake, yet treated as the one who could carry Macintosh to a bright future. He'd been set to receive leadership. Her father had said as much tonight when she'd lobbied for her and Drag's marriage. At the confirmation, she had executed the offer Cheatham had given her after the race. She'd dared to talk to him alone, but he'd liked her ambition, her guts.

Cheatham had smiled at her. His sly look would have been appealing to another woman. The devilish gleam in his eyes was more monstrous than attractive. *"Show me you mean it, prove your commitment to your future… Kill your father and his bastard."*

"Why Snapper?"

"Ask your father who he plans to let take over once you're married to me," Cheatham had replied.

She clenched her fist around the hilt of the blade. Her resolve had never been stronger. She'd been willing to give everything to the future she and Drag wanted. Her father and Snapper be damned. This would be over tonight and in the morning light she'd find solace in Drag's arms.

Believing that, she pushed onward to Snapper's hut and knocked on the door. Listening carefully, she heard no steps. He was probably asleep. The mechanic refrained from joining the parties, opting for rest instead, shunning traditions because he wasn't acknowledged by their father.

The door opened with no resistance, and she snuck into the room. Low light from a heat block on the far side of the room cast orangish-red shadows across the small space. She could make out the bulk of a figure on a cot against the wall. She crossed the room on her tiptoes and brought the knife up, ready to plunge it down.

"Bridget…what the hell?" Snapper's sleep-drowsy voice hit her ears.

She let the blade fall, putting as much momentum and force from her stance into the forward motion as she could.

"I'm sorry."

* * * *

Present day

"I'll represent us!" The booming voice Bridget didn't want to hear rose above the bulk of the group.

The hulking figure of her previous champion, Ironside, pushed his way to the forefront of the crowd. The dead white of his right eye was a stinging reminder of his last fight on her behalf. Ironside had been her father's closest friend, the one trusted with all the secrets, and when she'd taken over, she'd pushed him away, but not before he stood up to the man he'd believed had killed her father.

Ironside had been the one to cleave Drag's arm off, and with it his Macintosh ink. That had been twelve years ago. Now, Ironside was older. His black hair was streaked with gray and he was weathered and worn from going to work in the mines. Yet he still had a hulking figure that would intimidate most. No one challenged him to fight over anything—they just cleared the way. Ironside never had a reason to lie and was a staunch defender of their gang.

"You would be the one, too," Drag muttered.

Bridget stepped forward, half tempted to beg for another person. Ironside didn't deserve to sacrifice himself a second time and she had already watched him surrender enough.

She opened her mouth but shut it as others started to chant Ironside's name. The Inccukai met her gaze and cocked their head to the side in question. She shook her head. Trio wasn't a member of the gang and by that measure they couldn't interfere.

Small favor.

"You're going to let this go down?" Drag asked her. She barely heard his words over the recitation of Ironside's name. The older man with his scruffy beard was almost to the steps.

"I'm going to have to. The difference is now you have cybernetic parts and Ironside's up there in years."

"Where'd you dismiss him to after I was gone?"

"He took himself to the mines." Because she'd told Ironside the truth. She couldn't lie to him, not when he'd believed in her so damn much.

"You're fucking heartless, you know that?"

Bridget straightened up, tucking her hands into her vest pockets, and held herself high. *You're Bridget fucking Macintosh.* "So they say. But you wanted to make this a show. Go do it."

The words were out of her mouth from pure defiance but inside she was a crumbling wall weakened by time, a pure mess forcing herself not to give up. Her resolve was the one thing keeping her standing. The fact she couldn't let her guard diminish or show weakness in front of all these people bruised her deep inside. Tears couldn't even be shed for her father's best friend, who would allow himself to be killed in response to her cowardice all those years ago, when she'd been so afraid to speak the truth and be killed for her choices — choices she had made with the best interests of Macintosh in mind.

"Fine, but don't be upset when I kill the old man."

Ironside had reached them at that point, and he grinned at Drag. "I'm always eager for a new challenge. You weren't so hard to beat the first time, and I don't think your shiny new appendage is going to make that much difference."

The old man didn't spare her a second glance, which was as much as she deserved.

Drag crossed his arms and sunlight reflected off the metal. "You think so."

Ironside gave a nod. "I think that those who speak the truth and believe in their words with conviction to back them will win. As we all believe in Macintosh. Choose your weapon."

Bridget was back to all those years ago, when Drag had been thrown in the dirt in front of the dead bonfire pit on a hot Mars morning similar to this one, and told the same thing. Her heart had been in her throat, words unable to be summoned. Most believed it was in grief for her father's death and the betrayal that stung so bad.

Instead, she'd been torn by anger and fear, not wanting to lose Drag and at the same time so damn angry with him because he had refused to trust her and wanted to abandon their love.

"I don't need a weapon to take you on."

Those damn words were like a sharp blade straight to her heart. She adjusted her stance, trying to keep her posture relaxed. A few slow breaths in and out to reduce the sting.

"Fine, I'll take my ax. Like last time."

A true rematch in almost every way, except this time it wasn't about Drag wanting to prove Bridget was a murderer. Instead, he wanted to end their war and gain an alliance with them, help Macintosh rebuild.

"Then proceed to the pit," she forced herself to announce.

The crowd cheered. The bonfire pit was where they lit fires or fought duels. The pit held ashy remnants of the logs sacrificed. Their last party had been the night before the race as they had prayed that other opponents would be eliminated and let Macintosh into the championship. Though no such luck had occurred then, this duel also brought an opportunity.

If for some reason Drag died, Macintosh would be in the race. Would the next steps matter after that? *Yes, because Cheatham wants me as his wife.* Cheatham was tired of letting her play ruler, not when she could help in other ways. *Disgusting.*

Ironside and Drag reached the pit. Another Macintosh male handed Ironside his ax and he stepped within the metal-lined ring. Drag took off his hoodie to reveal a tan tank top underneath and tossed the sleeveless cover to Jack.

As he flexed, Drag's cybernetic arm sent another flash of light reflecting into the crowd. Bridget recalled Drag being fairly muscular back in the day, but he'd bulked up. His physique reminded her of statues, figures cut from rock that were immortalized at various racing domes on Mars.

Once again, she was thankful for the goggles that would keep her vision hidden from those watching. No one needed to see how affected she was by Drag's appearance. The tattoo of the Full Throttle symbol on his left arm was a stark reminder he hadn't been on Macintosh's side in a long time.

The pair circled each other at first, Ironside swinging his ax from side-to-side, then over the shoulder a bit as if to test the heft and showcase the power behind his swing. Drag watched, as if taking in the movements and saving them in his memory until later.

Bridget found her chest tight. She was almost unable to breathe, knowing what would come. Someone would get hurt, even possibly die. Like before, she wanted to cry out for them to stop this madness, but she was stuck riding this out until the very end, locked into traditions she despised and had been unable to change. A low chanting began among the group.

The calls for battle started low then rose, louder and louder until every member of Macintosh surrounding the pit ring clapped their hands together. The clash was real now and would be complete once one of them was on the ground.

Ironside immediately swung the ax. He had chosen a similar method of approach the first time. Brute force with little time for his opponent to think. But unlike the last fight, where Drag hadn't been sure if he wanted to fight back or not, this time Bridget saw determination in his eyes, the lockset of his jaw and the way he had fists at the ready. Instead of running, Drag moved in. He dodged the swing and the recoil, landing a punch with his human hand as he moved.

After Drag backed away, their movements were on repeat for a couple minutes. Ironside would try an attack, Drag would evade and return with a punch. His cybernetic hand was always at the ready but never in motion, which confused Bridget.

Is he trying to make this last a while?

If she'd been in there, her goal would have revolved around ending this as quick as she could. Each second it dragged on, the more her stomach rose into her throat, threatening to choke her from the anxiety. But she couldn't shout her recommendation. She wasn't supposed to want him to win, yet she did. His winning meant he'd be by her side again, on her side.

Stop living in a fantasy.

Her stupid attraction and deep-seated memories of the past wanted the fairy tale, even as she was aware he'd never fully trust her again. Another swing, a dodge, but this time Ironside sideswiped Drag with a backhand. The ax went flying to the edge of the circle. The older man was breathing heavy, his chest heaving up and down like the bellows on the fires in the forge to melt the marsanium.

Ironside was tired, but he had drawn blood. A thin trail trickled down from the crease of Drag's lip. The Full Throttle leader wiped it away then lunged, his patience for the drawn-out battle melting away. Drag let his cybernetic fist fly. The crunch of bones against unyielding metal was heard loud and clear. Several groans and pained gasps came from the crowd.

Bridget held her breath as Ironside fell at first to one knee.

Drag didn't hesitate but swept the older man's other leg, dropping the former first lieutenant of Macintosh flat on his face, his salt and pepper hair covering his eyes.

Ironside had to have said something because Drag crouched down next to him. She couldn't see Ironside's lips, but something was being exchanged. Drag nodded then gave a single punch to the man's neck, crushing his spine right where it met the back of his head.

The shock in the crowd propelled Bridget forward. She had to ensure this went the way she wanted it to and prevent a riot from breaking out. As the voices of dissent began, she could sense the Inccukai making their move.

No…not today.

She jumped into the ring beside Drag, moving faster than she'd ever done before. She swallowed hard and summoned the courage to sound strong, resolute. *You are Bridget fucking Macintosh.*

"It appears justice has spoken. The Full Throttle leader's words ring true, by him winning the contest. I will accept his victory and his promise to Macintosh. Do you follow my way?"

Chapter Six

If someone had told Drag his ex-lover who had tried to kill him twelve years ago would be standing beside him in the town they grew up in backing his actions and words, he'd have laughed in their face. Such things were the stuff of dreams.

Yet here Bridget was beside him, announcing her backing. He momentarily looked up from his crouched spot, where her bright auburn hair glimmered in the sunlight. He'd opted to go without sun goggles, so his view was a little shadowed as he kept his gaze away from the sun shining in the sky above.

"Does this mean no war?" a member of the crowd shouted.

"Correct. We are no longer at war. I will listen to what Drag offers and work out details with him." She leaned down and tugged on his human arm, forcing him to come to his feet. "We leave you now. Take care of Ironside and we will celebrate his passing this evening with a bonfire send-off."

Then she moved, marching out of the pit and back up the steps. Drag took one last glance at Ironside. The old man had begged for him to end it, leaving Drag confused, because besides asking Drag to take his life, Ironside had also asked that Drag take care of Bridget.

The same Bridget that was already halfway to her front door. Drag moved to catch up and gave Jack a shrug. Jack motioned toward the house, a silent question of whether he should follow. Drag shook his head. In case things went sour, he'd need a quick getaway.

He also didn't miss the Inccukai who was at Ironside's body and inspecting the damage Drag had inflicted. *Hopefully, the mummy gets the point.*

Drag wasn't sure if he could fight them, but he didn't mind being seen as a threat. Most people were unaware of how much strength he and his cybernetic friends possessed. Today he'd displayed a fraction of it, though a thread of guilt still ran through his system for ending Ironside. He'd known the old lieutenant since he was a kid. The man had always served beside Travis Macintosh as his second until the leader's death.

Bridget was already inside the house and Drag stopped himself short, recalling the last time he'd walked through the door. It had been the beginning of the end of everything between them.

Will this be the start of something new?

He couldn't let those fantasies resurface. This place represented childhood dreams of youth, lost twelve years ago. Sweeping back the thick curtain that served as a door, he entered. The lighting inside was horribly dim. It took a couple seconds for his eyes to adjust, then he caught sight of Bridget on the far side of the room in the kitchen area. She already had a bottle of recycle and a kit of supplies on the table.

"Take a seat," she said before crossing the room to get a bowl.

He made it to the table and hesitated over the chair she'd pulled out. "What's all this for?"

She sighed, then kicked his left boot before clamping a hand on his left shoulder to force him down. He went with the motion and plopped into the chair, the wood creaking and screeching under his weight and the pressure of the small slide against the wood-grain floor.

"You're bleeding above your eye and there's a cut on your arm."

He opened his mouth to retort that she didn't need to worry. Cybernetics would have him healed within an hour. But instead, he shut up and let her start to work on him. Her hands were calloused, not smooth like he remembered, and those mouth-bitten nails the opposite of her preferences. Her skin tan and mottled with freckles, scars, on the backs near her wrists. She'd even broken one finger, judging by the weird set to it.

What the hell has she been doing?

She doused a clean cloth with some liquid and he couldn't help the tiny hiss from the sting when she touched the solution to the cut above his eye. She repeated the steps on his arm.

"You weren't making it look good out there. At all," she said.

"I'm sitting here bleeding and you're complaining about my performance. I won. That's all that matters."

"You killed him," she mumbled as she grabbed a small bandage and the tape, ripping a piece off the roll with her teeth. Tears were gathering at the corner of her eyes and regardless of the rage that had briefly overtaken him in the bonfire pit, remorse clamped down hard on his chest now.

"Hey, I didn't have a choice…besides, you sent him to the mines."

The tape roll dropped in the bowl with a clink. She sniffled a couple times, avoiding his gaze. "I know…but it doesn't mean this hurts less."

"If it helps at all, I'm sorry." He'd always be upset to put any type of distress on her features. Realizing that in this moment sucked so damn much. He tried to grasp at the anger all over again, but the fury was weak in the face of her tear-stained cheeks.

After applying the bandage, she gave his arm a slap. The sting was so minor he didn't react at all. No, he was too busy looking at her face.

Those eyebrows, the freckles, the green of her irises trained on his arms and the way she struggled to hold a small grin on those lips… Lips he wanted to know if they still kissed the same. Stupid for sure, but the desire was there and if it mean she'd stop being sad…

She started to pull back and he reached for her, easily wrapping his thick hand around her thin forearm. Time had stolen from her, removed some of the meat to her bones and erased the pampered princess parts he'd once found himself attracted to. Their time apart had hardened her.

"What?" she asked, her gaze at last resting on his.

"Why are you taking the time to clean me up?"

She gave a half shrug, unable to move her right side as easily with him holding onto her. "Seemed like the right thing to do."

"You going to hold a grudge because I killed Ironside?" The question paired with him pulling her closer to him.

Real smooth, Drag… Talk about a dead guy.

"No, he asked you to, right?"

"Protect her, keep her safe."

Those were the words Ironside left with him, his last ones before Drag got a front row seat to the life fading from his eyes. Sure, he felt bad and at the same time satisfied with delivering well-earned payback since the old man had taken his arm twelve years prior.

"He did. Still, you're upset and I don't want all this work to go to waste."

The visual struggle taking place in front of him was a marvel to see. Bridget sat up straight, eyes flashing with momentary frustration, followed by the exact opposite. He wasn't sure what had prompted her reaction, but as fast as she aimed for attack, all the bravado disappeared. She slouched in the chair and looked up to the ceiling.

"Would it still make sense if I said I'm glad you weren't hurt again?"

Fuck. The words, almost a whisper from her lips, sliced through him worse than any damage he'd sustained in the last decade because of how badly he wanted her to be telling the truth.

It took a small yank and she was standing between his legs, her hands resting on his shoulders. Looking down at him, she licked her lips. That was it—he was fucking done. Hadn't Snapper warned him about this? For thirty seconds, he wouldn't fucking care.

Let me forget.

He reached up, cupping the back of her head and pulling her face toward his. "Now's the time to slap me and pull back."

"Can I touch you? Because I want to kiss bad enough to break the rules," she growled in return.

He found himself nodding without hesitation, so she moved in. For the first time in twelve years, a strange sense of right washed over him as her lips met his.

A girl should know how to play hard to get, but in this situation Bridget didn't. She hadn't been lying when she said her heart mourned for Ironside but had been thankful Drag was alive.

Now she was kissing him in her kitchen, and it didn't take much to move from a simple embrace to threading her fingers through his hair. Then he touched a tongue to her lips and she opened, not even attempting to hold herself back. She'd been without this for so long and Drag... *No one's ever kissed me like Dakota Michelson.*

He was teasing her into a frenzy, pulling her tightly against him and plundering her mouth like a miner attacking a good vein of ore. This rough part of him, the way he took over and used her, had her damp between her legs and, like a sex-starved moron, contemplating how far could she let this go. How much did she dare?

Beyond tangling tongues and the nipping bites he gave to her lips, he traced out the inside of her mouth as if trying to map her and lay possessive claim in one fell swoop. This was what she'd wished for her in her dreams and those dark nights alone.

When he let her go, she was breathing heavy and wishing there wasn't a crowd still outside awaiting news of their alliance.

"I *wish* you'd just listened to me back then. This wouldn't have ended." She was immediately stumbling backward as Drag shoved himself out of the chair to a full standing position. Regret coiled in her chest. The words were far too candid and by the intensity of Drag's frown, not the best ones.

"You tried to kill my best friend... Listening to you would have been a horrible idea."

I had reasons.

"I thought I was your best friend. Remember the promise you made to me."

Drag shook his head. "No, you broke all of those when you became a killer. You took our future into your hands and snapped it in two."

"He would have been named leader. I couldn't let that happen." No, not when it would mean losing the hold over Cheatham. Though after twelve years she stood atop the same precipice after all. "Forget it. Let's not dwell on the past anymore. We're here to talk the future."

He grabbed the chair, turned it around so the back faced her then sat again. "To be clear, my head was a little confused after the fight. Adrenaline...that's what inspired the kiss. We're not doing that again, or anything else for that matter."

She sat down and crossed her legs, willing her desire to disappear completely. "Of course, like I said. We're focusing on the alliance."

Alliance, right. Focus.

Drag was anything but clear headed. He was aroused and angry at Bridget for acting as if their downfall had resided in his inability to do as she'd asked, when their split was due to her being a murderous, power-hungry person. He'd thought her beyond despot behavior, but she'd proven otherwise.

Add in Ironside's comment and he was confused. The man had been treated abominably by Bridget after beating him and sending him from Macintosh. Yet the old man still believed that somehow Bridget needed to be kept safe.

"Shall we begin?" she asked, busying herself by packing up the supplies on the table and putting them back in the box.

"I delivered my side of the bargain — we're no longer at war. Now it's time to dig into your plan. How are we keeping that Inccukai out of your business as well?" He stretched his arms out before tearing off the bandage she had put over his eye.

She growled, then gasped softly. "Where the hell did your injury go?"

"One of the perks of being a cyborg is faster healing abilities."

"You could have mentioned that before wasting my time," she murmured, her words barely audible over the squeak of the metal-hinged door and clasping lock on the repair kit.

He grinned. "When would I ever turn down a woman who wanted to spend time fawning over me?"

"Typical...anyway. The next step is recon. We're going to have to infiltrate the racing dome. With the impending championship, Cheatham is going to be here and how we prove to the others of what he's capable of is we get him caught on record talking about his plans. That's not even exploring who on the commission he has in his pocket."

The words hit Drag and he recoiled. "Wait? You're saying someone on the commission is taking payments from Cheatham?"

"You didn't think he did all of this by himself, did you?" Bridget let out a little chuckle, grating against Drag's already exposed nerves.

"I never believed they were corrupted."

She shook her head. "Well, pity on you. There is always someone willing to sacrifice the benefits of others for a chance at more ways to line their own pockets and I'm seeing it more and more."

"You cashed in on some of that yourself, right?"

The frown on her face mirrored the frustration brewing within him. She acted as if she abhorred the behavior, but she'd killed her own father to be placed in leadership. Would have killed Snapper too, if Drag hadn't stopped her, then made how many deals... *Hypocrisy.*

"I secured my future. You just couldn't grasp that I was fighting for what we wanted."

Bullshit. "We're not talking about the past. I'm saying now. Are you taking payoffs to make deals and do shit you're not supposed to? Or are things like blowing up my racer and driver or sending a spy into my gang all you?" He couldn't help but ask the questions he'd wanted to for months.

"Will those answers make it better?" Snapper had shared those words with him when he'd suggested this morning that maybe this alliance would get them an explanation for Bridget's violence against them.

I need to hear them.

"Why does that matter?"

"It's going to ensure I don't walk away from this alliance."

She sighed. "You're not going to trust me regardless, but fine. I was challenged by Cheatham to ensure we won. I bribed one person to get into your pit area and plant that bomb. When we didn't succeed... Well, he's going to remove me from leadership. I said this already."

Were the ideas yours? He wanted to ask, but Snapper was right. Her answers wouldn't make him feel any better or improve things. They would serve as a reminder of why a future between them was never possible.

"Fine. How sure are you that this infiltration and setting up surveillance equipment is going to get us any traction? People who do bad things aren't considered stupid enough to get caught. They won't just talk about dirty dealings in the middle of a room."

"You'd be surprised, Drag. These idiots are starting to feel comfortable in their positions and believe they are invincible. They don't think anyone capable of attempting such a thing. I've often heard those on the commission and even the sponsors enjoy it when there is infighting within gangs in the territories. Hell, some have been trying to stoke the fires of the unaffiliated groups to cause more anarchy, if anything. The chaos allows them to get away with decisions and choices they would never try if people were bothering to pay attention."

Drag couldn't fault her knowledge. As a leader struggling with a gang on the brink of starvation and failure, he'd been more focused on the people he answered to than attending commission meetings or paying attention to the bullshit politics running Mars as a whole.

"Then they need to be removed."

She shrugged. "Maybe. I'm not sure how deep the corruption goes. I have some ideas, but I want proof to share with the other leaders. That's the only way we get anywhere in this system. We need unity across Mars, across all the gangs. To show the commissions they represent us, are elected by us. And if the Smiths pull off parliament representation one day, we need a better voice."

"Didn't know you were a fan of politics?" He couldn't help but chide her, because these words were reminiscent of the woman he'd loved twelve years prior. A person he'd wanted to help change their world, but who had instead turned into a monster. The very creatures she wanted to fight against.

"My father always said it came with the territory. The problem was he didn't believe women were smart enough to be involved in the workings. I may never have a chance to prove him wrong, but I won't be forced into a corner again."

Those words rang out to him as odd. The Bridget he'd always known made her own choices, which was why her father's murder and the near killing of Snapper were so shocking. He thought he knew the real her, but those events had him questioning his very sanity.

"All right, how do we get in?"

"The prelim walk-through, in one week. We'll need your tech-savvy mechanic's help. The female with the fancy skills."

He raised an eyebrow. "Do you have another spy in my gang?"

"Wouldn't you like to know?" She chuckled. "No, Drag. But it doesn't take a genius to discover she's become the brains of your operation. She was the mind behind splitting the sludge from the NiteOx and combusting it outside the chamber. There's a half a dozen mechanics wishing they'd thought of the same thing. I'm sure she's adept at cameras, sensors and spy shit."

Gina, in truth an AI and not human, was capable of far more. But Drag would never admit as much out loud. Gina had trusted him, as she done the same for a few in Full Throttle, with the knowledge of her true nature. He'd die to protect her because she'd offered his gang so much and because his best friend loved the woman more than he cared for his own life.

"She may have some skill in that area."

"She'd need to, especially since she helped you steal from half a dozen gangs. Stop looking at me like that. I'm not stupid, Drag, no matter what you may think of me. I pay attention to things, including the tiny details that most people would overlook."

He needed to stop narrowing his scope to his gang as a whole, if her observations told him anything. First thing when he got back, Gina would need to run a security analysis of Frog Lick. No more leaving things to chance. Two hours in this woman's company and he was becoming paranoid.

"Maybe I should be concerned that you're stalking me." He tried to shake off his concern with a joke and a smile.

"Drag, if I was hunting you, you'd know. I'm not a fan of hiding in the dark."

Chapter Seven

Bridget fidgeted in the hauler as it blasted across the rocky Mars terrain, the desert-sparse vegetation dotting the horizon, along with the hulking figure of the racing dome. It dominated the bulk majority of the landscape and wasn't far from Frog Lick.

Her mind trailed to Drag, who she hadn't seen in a week, though as promised, he'd sent a courier in the form of Jack and his woman, Shannon. They'd come bearing gifts — knowledge to increase their water filtration production and supplies to build a second tank, along with some seeds and instructions to provide to those Drag had known as growers.

It appeared Full Throttle wasn't starving as had been previously predicted. They were thriving with the help of farming and cultivating the harsh landscape. Bridget had been jealous of those developments when she'd first learned of them.

Those were her days of anger, when she'd wanted Drag to suffer, along with Snapper, the latter being who she'd blamed for taking Drag away from her. They'd received matching wounds, lost arms, but had managed to survive.

Fucking Smiths. Bebe had taken them in and made them even better, thanks to the cybernetic testing. Bridget had never gotten her revenge, another thing working against her. As everyone around her suffered, her ex-lover had thrived. Bebe had been arrested for some bullshit plot, which Bridget had hailed and believed that maybe Drag and the others would be included.

Except no—instead Drag had become Full Throttle's leader, changing the gang name and her future. He was the bane of her existence and now she'd agreed to work alongside him, tempting herself even further.

"You're quiet today," Trio said in a quiet voice next to her ear. They sat in the backseat behind her.

She'd been so deep in contemplation she hadn't felt the damn assassin sneak in next to her. She preferred far more distance between them, even if that didn't matter. If Cheatham gave orders to have her removed, it wouldn't take more than a minute, and no amount of space between them would prevent the killer from completing their job.

"A lot on my mind."

"Anything to do with a certain gang leader? You know my contract holder will never agree to whatever he's planning here."

She fucking knew, but what that asshole permitted or not wouldn't matter if they got him recorded trying to run one of his dirty schemes. That was the end game she needed to keep working toward. She'd have Cheatham by the balls then, and he'd have to back off and leave her alone.

"All I'm concerned about is the advantages he can bring to Macintosh. We're already well benefited by the alliance. We keep them close, and then when they've given us everything, we end things."

"So, you'd fuck him then?"

She coiled her fists in her lap. "That's none of your damn business. It's none of your boss' either."

"He doesn't want you soiled."

Keeping her eyes on the ever-growing dome in front of them she took a calming breath because what she said next could impact how things played out. "I'll say this again—I'll sleep with who I want, when I want. If he doesn't like it, he can take care of the problem himself. You lay a hand on anyone who touches me, and I'll make sure you're denied everywhere in Macintosh. Special privileges gone, and be sure you can wander the territories trying to find a place to hide. You don't threaten me. Ever."

The damn assassin laughed, loud and unfamiliar. Bridget hadn't heard this head-to-toe-covered creature laugh or even eat. The Inccukai were in general people who inspired fear—augmented bodies that were once adapted bodyguards for parliament. In the not-so-distant past, their order had lost the parliament contract and been disbanded. Those assassins who couldn't hack it with mere existence and loved killing often found work with cartels and others who were willing to pay their fees. Those folks didn't care how many dead bodies were left in the path of their goals.

"I find it enjoyable when you try to pretend you're tough. You've killed one person…doesn't make you capable."

My father, you bastard. She still had nightmares from that awful moment. But she'd been so sure of her conviction it hadn't mattered when she'd been executing the deed. But when she'd been abandoned and alone...different story.

"I've ordered the destruction of plenty of others, testing their resolve and yours. Don't tempt me."

The driver let out a cough, and Bridget was aware they had an audience, but she'd ensure the stories he had to tell involved the Macintosh leader not pulling any punches. She'd give as hard as anyone.

"You think you'd have a chance?"

At one point she'd wanted a friendship from this jerk, but Trio always did a good job of disabusing the notion she could trust them. "I might get taken out, but I'd take at least a piece of you while I went."

They passed through the gates of the racing dome and into the underground parking area for visitors. There were several other haulers entering as well.

Trio leaned in closer again. "I'd like to see that one day. I'll steer clear for now, but if your work threatens Cheatham's ultimate goals, I will have to take action."

"We'll see." She refused to concede. This was probably the one time she'd been at odds with Trio. They'd been reluctant allies over the last five years. When Macintosh had been threatened by another gang, Cheatham had sent the assassin to ensure his holdings weren't threatened. The assassin hadn't wanted to be here anymore than she wanted them, but they'd worked together...until now. Their goals didn't align with hers, not anymore.

Bridget recognized haulers from Singh, Osprerine, Gemino, Silva-Chavez and Skeiron. Her gaze tracked across the garage space. The lighting wasn't the greatest, with recycled solar tracks outlining the ceiling with random strands in various geometric shapes, similar to how the tube lighting in the mines was set up, with varying success.

She didn't spot the Full Throttle hauler, with their tell-tale checkered flag symbol. Maybe he wouldn't come. It was entirely possible he had changed his mind. This was a big risk, but without their help, she'd never pull it off.

The rumble of a couple haulers could be heard in the distance, and she angled herself in her seat so she could see the entrance with ease. Damn Trio for watching her so close, but the temptation to seek Drag out was too great for her to ignore. *Remember, he has to come.*

They were the champions and had to show for the prelim walk-through. The ceremony requirements, the details...there had to be representatives on hand. The commission wouldn't let them race without being present.

The first hauler that zoomed in wasn't Full Throttle, but she recognized the Aurestral leaders, husband and wife. Half the man's body was covered in cybernetics, evidence of her poor choices. *My fault that.* The hauler was backed up by a second and third hauler. These were Full Throttle. Drag and Jack rode in the first, along with Snapper and Gina in the second. Her half-brother was here... *Great.*

As if she didn't have plenty of enemies to contend with, this one added another wrinkle. Gathering her feelings and stuffing them down, she pulled herself up via the overhead bar and shoved her body out of the vehicle. Forget opening a door, she wanted a bigger entrance. Drag's hauler came to a stop right next to her, inches from running over her toes. Both Drag and Jack were grinning at her, knowing damn well the proximity to her feet.

"Surprises me with your inability to drive how you ever got into the championship round."

"Well, that's not me. Jack is behind the wheel, but he figured you might be due a reminder of how easy it is to lose an appendage." Drag, similar to her, hefted himself out of the hauler without even opening a door.

Bridget couldn't stop her feet from moving, meeting him at the back of the haulers. Her mind was caught up in how good he looked, though he wore a dark-colored T-shirt, standard cargo style pants many racers wore and the boots. He'd shaved his face, though — no scruff. She wanted to touch those cheekbones, feel the smoothness that would be gone by the late afternoon.

"You ready for this?"

He grinned, his gaze trailing the length of her body and back up. "Oh, talking about my talented driving skills, no. I'll let Snapper handle all the racing details."

She'd briefly forgotten her half-brother until now. "Sure he can be trusted with that kind of importance?"

"Far more than you could be with anything," Snapper replied, coming to stand beside Drag. He had his arm around the shoulders of a woman almost the same height as he. They both had a couple inches on her.

The blonde, Gina, had a strange purple color to her irises, one Bridget found a little arresting and she couldn't help but continue to cast glances back and forth between the three of them. She was surprised Drag had let such a beauty escape his notice. The woman would have looked amazing on his arm.

On her half-brother's… Well, she could barely look at him, because outside of coloring, Snapper looked just like her father. She saw his prompting gaze, the question of why reflected back to her if she dared to stare at him.

"That remains to be seen," she offered in reply. "If you ever want to rid yourself of him, let me know." This she said to Gina.

The woman smiled at her, a polite nod, but her eyes were staring daggers. "Believe me, I'd rid him of you before the opposite would happen."

So, Snapper had found someone he cared enough about to tell her who Bridget was, and what she'd done.

"You're lucky you found one to stay loyal to you," Bridget replied off-handedly as others were starting to gather several feet away. They didn't need an audience. "What do you plan to do?"

"Take in the track, a little fresh air. Care to join me?" Drag asked.

There were looks given, glances that spoke volumes. She sensed the Inccukai and her driver watching nearby. Could she avoid the meeting?

"Don't worry, my crew will get all the important details. There won't be anything needing decision-making input right away so you can come with me." Drag held out his hand and she couldn't breathe for a moment.

Surrounded by enemies and people judging her, how could she take his hand? That would be like announcing to everyone they were more than just allies, right? *Stop it, he's giving you a cover story to be sneaking around without anyone watching.*

She slipped her hand into his, enjoying how warm his palm was, the calluses rubbing against hers. They were alike in ways. He tugged her toward him and she went. But instead of wrapping her against his body, he started walking toward the field. She wasn't sure what to say, if she should object or let things continue.

He spoke before she could. "We're going sightseeing. Take good notes and tell them we'll join them for the meeting at the end."

Her steps were brisk and double what Drag was putting down, just to keep up with him. He still had a hold of her and that was enough to send her heart into double-time beating. They were almost to the other entrance to the garage where it opened up into the track, allowing sightseers to enter as they chose, when Bridget dared to speak.

"Just like that, you expect them to do as you say."

"I expected them to take care of your Inccukai and use them as a representative for you."

"Don't we need Gina?" she asked, pulling her sun goggles up on her forehead. Inside the dome they had enough protection to not need them.

"I've got the supplies in my pockets. Don't worry, she gave me good instructions. We'll be fine."

Bridget should have known they would be walking into this place with a plan. "What about the guards?"

"We already mapped their schedule. Why do you think I'm walking so fast?"

She chuckled. "Because you want to get me alone."

"I mean...that's what it's looking like to everyone else. Just as planned."

Drag released Bridget's hand when they were out of eyesight from the group in the garage. Snapper, Gina and Jack had their directions—keep the damn Inccukai away from them while Drag and Bridget would assume the risk of installing the cameras that Gina had built the last couple of days.

They were small, but with a wide-scope lens and the ability to pick up a pin drop. Drag had been concerned the AI female had been spying on them with this tech, but she'd sworn on her love for Snapper she'd never do that.

"Why are we doing this and not Gina and Snapper?"

He figured Bridget would ask. "Because no way is my crew assuming the hazard for your big scheme. We are in this together and I believe that if you're not willing to do the job yourself, then you shouldn't risk others."

This was part of his commitment to his family. He would put himself in danger first before imperiling them. It was the best way to handle this threat. Because Bridget was nothing if not a danger to all of them, he'd rather assume the gamble instead of passing it on to someone else.

"Fair enough. But where are you taking me? The meeting rooms are back with the whole group. We might have had more luck just going to the damn walk-through."

Drag shook his head. "We have that schedule, too. We're going to start with the commission offices, then move into the others. We have to be quick."

"How many guards and how often?"

Drag sensed her slowing her steps so he reached for her arm this time and tugged at her to keep up with him. "About a two dozen with rotating shifts every thirty solar minutes. Enough time to squeeze in but I'm keeping the schedules in my head right now, so I need you to move fast."

He found her proximity a bit of a double-edged blade, both enjoying her reliance on him and despising it. She looked damn hot, too, with her pants and that tight shirt and vest pushing her breasts up so he got a glimpse of those smooth mounds lightly dusted in freckles.

She's been sunning again.

They'd joked about that often. How she'd be freckled all over if she kept exposing skin to the sun instead of protecting it.

"Fine, you're already leading the way. No sense in me trying to stop you."

They were stealth and quiet personified as they made their way up the stairs around the seating in the dome to the second level where the gang leader and guest boxes were, followed by another couple flights to the third level of the dome, near the top, where the commission had offices, meeting rooms and other entertaining areas.

He'd only been up to this level a handful of times, for verdicts and approvals to allow his gang to keep racing. After the mess Bebe Smith had left Full Throttle in, he'd had to fight tooth and nail to get them to approve the racing, even as they cut Full Throttle off at the balls by taking away their ability to build ships.

Reaching the top, Drag pried open a door with brute strength to get them inside the glass-covered area. They entered a dim hallway. Strips of light highlighted the floor to guide the way. The others would have taken a lift to the same level and would be meeting in a room to the right. So, they'd be headed left. The diagram displayed a group of six offices meant for both the racing and shipping commission. They had similar accommodations at the other racing domes, but favored Wespero as a home base, for various reasons. Nicer climate conditions, central location and for some reason those from the Uppers always preferred to come to this area.

With the championship less than a few weeks away, all commission members would make this dome their central hub for the foreseeable future.

Drag crept down the left hallway, keeping an eye out for guards, Bridget right beside him. Then she wasn't. He stopped and looked around, tracking her down. She'd stopped about three feet back and was staring at the holo-images being broadcast on the wall.

"Bridget," he harshly whispered. "There's no time for sightseeing on this trip."

When she didn't answer, he had no choice but to double back. If they were caught all this clandestine bullshit would be over before it really began.

He came to a stop beside her and nudged her arm. "What the hell is up with you?"

"My father." She pointed to the image and that was when he noticed the tears streaming down her face.

Sympathy blossomed, unwanted and unasked for, but he still felt something for this woman who was hurt by what she had lost. *Though she's the reason he's gone…* The retort sat on the tip of his tongue, and he swallowed hard to hold it back. Anything he said wouldn't change what had happened or make her soften toward him.

"If we don't move in the next thirty seconds, we're going to get caught." He spoke low, next to her ear and didn't miss the way she shivered. Her physical reaction to him would never not light him on fire.

"Let's go." She pushed past him and started to jog. Her steps still silent and he fell in beside her as they moved at quick clip toward their destination.

"Second door on the left up ahead. The Slither etched into the door."

Bridget got there first, only because Drag didn't want a repeat of her walk down memory lane. Better to keep her in his sight. She tried the door with no luck. Before Drag could show off his breaking and entering skills, Bridget was pulling a set of lock-picking keys from her vest pockets and getting to work.

"How much time?" she asked.

"Five seconds before those guards start doing a hall sweep."

"You'd think they'd install cameras, like we're planning to do."

Drag let out a half-snort, half-chuckle then whispered, "Yeah, the leaders would never agree to it. The idea of these commissions is based on mutual trust. We start spying on everyone, then the faith in this fucked-up system fades away."

The lock clicked beneath Bridget's hands, and she pushed the door open. Drag could already hear the footsteps of the guards and crowded in close, shoving Bridget's crouched form through the entrance. She surprisingly didn't collapse in a heap but dropped into a rolling position as Drag got himself inside. The door shut and locked before she could give him hell.

The marching cadence of the guards kept her from speaking, even as she popped up into a standing position. She stood there, hands on her hips, hitting him with a narrow-eyed glower, though her fierce gaze melted away as the guards came to a stop and checked the door, jiggling the handle. They moved on when it didn't give way and Drag let out the breath he was holding.

"What next?" Bridget whispered as she motioned to the room around them.

"We set up the cameras." Drag took note of the floor layout and moved toward the desk. There were some ideal spots that he recalled from Gina's instructional session.

"One under the desk, for audio purposes. Then try to place one in each corner from the desk facing toward the door. Best to see who is coming in the room and what they are giving the commissioner."

He pulled out a chair and waved his hand for Bridget to come closer. The chair itself didn't appear the sturdiest and wouldn't work with his weight.

"You stand on the chair, and I'll hand you the camera. It's just a peel-and-stick job."

"With my fingerprints on them?"

Drag pulled out the first camera and rubbed his human index finger along the back. "Mine are there now too. Happy?"

"Not really. That chair doesn't look safe."

He lifted it up then plopped it right next to the nearest corner. "You'll have more success than me."

She put one foot in the seat, then the other, clamping a hand on his shoulder for leverage as she lifted herself into the chair. His instinct was to put a steadying hand on her waist...his human one holding the pin-sized camera.

"Hand me the camera."

He offered it to her and tried to repress the electric reaction he experienced when her fingers touched his. It was like the jolt he'd experienced when his cybernetics got to close to a live wire—exhilarating and too damn risky.

She positioned the camera in the corner. "Right here?"

"That works. Take the backing off and stick it."

She did as he instructed, then they repeated the step in the next corner. Didn't take long to place the last one. From there they were on to the next office, with six in total. Two from each territory, with three sitting on the racing commission, and three on the mining and building commission. These were the representatives of the gangs as a form of government. They each served for a limited time.

They'd reached the last office, the one belonging to the commissioner of Wespero for the racing commission, a man from Singh called Paulos. Paulos had been instrumental in helping ensure their racer competed without disqualification, especially when they'd started using NiteOx. The true genius lay with Gina, but still, without this commissioner's willingness to hear them out and have a demonstration, they might never have had the opportunity at a championship.

Hell, Drag almost felt guilty for even putting cameras in this office.

"I don't think this is our culprit, but I get it, leave no stone unturned, no chance untaken."

Bridget nodded in agreement. "Correct. I mean, you thought you could trust me and see how easy I fell. It could happen to anyone."

"*Protect her.*"

Ironside's words came back to haunt him again. Not like the old man's dying visage weren't already haunting his dreams. He helped Bridget onto the chair, she placed the camera and somehow as she stepped backward, she slipped.

One second, he'd been supporting her by the waist and the next she was collapsing into his arms, the chair sliding out from underneath and crashing against the floor. Bridget's chest heaved up and down. He cradled her in his cybernetic hand. With his human one, he brushed the hair out of her face.

"Are you all right?"

"Fine," she whispered back.

Her eyes were on his lips, and it was just like back in her kitchen. The world was falling away and all he could see was her green-colored gaze, the light blush across her cheeks and those damn kissable lips begging for him.

"Do it," she demanded.

He half wanted to tease her about how she'd become much more commanding since he'd left. To the point he longed to make her beg for it.

"Ask me for permission."

She sighed, her body shimmying in his hold, restless. "Please, let me touch you."

"Tell me how bad you want me." The words were out of his mouth before he could stop them.

"I touched myself last night thinking about you. About the kitchen. And your mouth."

Fuck it.

He crashed his lips against hers, licking the seam, forcing his way inside when she didn't open immediately. That was her way of playing, to beg for him then battle in return. But no matter, the moan she let out told him he'd made the right choice. The kiss deepened and that was when the lock at the door clicked and the door opened with a good whoosh of air.

"Freeze!"

Chapter Eight

Drag pulled Bridget away after the protectorate guards yelled out. Irritation mingled with the arousal coursing through her veins. This was the second damn time she'd been in the middle of a kiss with this man and something had interrupted them.

"Get the hell out of here," Bridget responded back, unable to lock down her frustration.

She was horny and tired of not being able to take this further, even if doing so would be foolish as hell. *Fool's my middle name.* At this point, she'd made enough poor choices to decide that one more wasn't going to change the trajectory of her life. If anything, maybe Drag could infuse a little luck into her.

"You've broken into a commissioner's office and therefore have broken the law."

"The door was unlocked, and I think I'd be breaking some common decency laws if I fucked her in the hallway," Drag fired back.

He was staring straight in her eyes as he spoke, and she didn't miss the brief flash of desire that appeared when he spoke crudely. Those words reminded her of other ones, ones he hadn't called her in so long. Turns of phrase she'd dreamed about on lonesome nights where not even her hand could take away the ache.

The guards grumbled amongst themselves before one spoke up. "Just hurry up and finish."

"I'm not a fan of performing with an audience…at least not sexual acts."

"Fucking drivers," the guard murmured. The other chuckled, situation diffused, but not Bridget's arousal. She bit her lip to keep from echoing her earlier words. *They need to leave. Now.*

"Fine. If you're here on our next rotation check, we're arresting you for breaking and entering. I don't give a flying winged hoot if she's the greatest lay in Wespero." The door shut, footsteps walked in the other direction and Bridget let her head fall back against the floor.

"That was too damn close."

"Yeah…but damn if that didn't make this a little more exciting." Drag grinned at her and she recalled how much of an adrenaline junkie he'd been in their years growing up. Getting chased, racing, fucking somewhere they might almost get caught… It was always a game to him.

"Do you think you can still work magic in fifteen minutes?"

His grin turned downright feral. "I can do one better, but only if you ask nicely, like a good girl would."

A shiver slithered down her spine, her nerve-endings like live wires and her panties were soaked.

Two little words and he reduced her to nothing and everything.

"Pretty please, make me come."

That was all he needed to hear to spring into action—his mouth was on hers in a flash, followed by his fingers at her buttons. No foreplay, no joking. He was in serious action mode working her pants and panties down just enough.

"I can't spread my legs," she mumbled against his lips.

He licked her and chuckled. "That's the point. Hold onto my head and don't dare make a noise. Otherwise, you won't be a good girl, and we all know what happens when good girls are naughty."

"I'll behave."

He slid down her body, passing up her aching nipples hard as points underneath her vest and shirt. No, he opted to go straight for the patch of red hair between her legs. He paused there, as she kept her fingers tethered in his hair. A breath against her heated flesh made her shiver. Then he used his thumbs to spread her lips just enough that her clit was exposed.

"You're so beautiful. Look at your clit all erect and ready for me." Drag dipped a finger lower, toward her entrance, and coated it in her essence. She was dripping at this point, but at his mercy and couldn't say anything. She wanted to come and be damned if her release got withheld because she couldn't follow a couple directions. *I'm a naughty girl, after all.*

He gave the first lick, and she clenched her fists in his hair. The second one and her legs went stiff involuntarily. When was the last time she'd let someone go down on her? *Never...* Not in twelve years, because that would be too close to what she'd enjoyed with Drag. Having this again was like a dream she didn't want to wake up from. She bit her lip as he kept working her.

Then he'd pause and speak sweet nothings. "I'm going to make you come just this way, licking your clit. You're going to be quiet, right?"

He glanced up from his position at the apex of her thighs and all she could do was nod.

"Good girl. After I'm done, you're going to walk around all day with your panties soaked, thinking about what I did for you."

Then he was back at it, flicks and licks, his attention to detail astounding. Where most men wanted to just slip a dick in her, Drag was focused on making her orgasm in such a way she'd be thinking about it for days.

Her entire body was now speeding down a course toward completion that he commanded, the same way he drove a racer, with precision and maneuverability very few possessed. And he already knew her body, the little ways he could twist his tongue against her to cause her to squirm.

"You're so close, aren't you?" He whispered the question in between ministrations.

"Yes, please... Please, Dakota..." She almost told him to make her his but stopped herself short. She'd even resorted to his birth name, not the one denoted to him.

He sucked the hood of her clit into his mouth then flicked it with his tongue. That was enough to trigger a cascade of release, her legs locked and her frame rigid underneath him as her orgasm coated her.

"You can let go of my hair now."

She did as he asked, and he pushed himself upward using his palms until he was crouched over her.

"That's a good girl. Now lift your ass, so I can get these clothes back on you. We have a few minutes left before we have to get out of here."

She arched up as much as she could and Drag put her pants back in order. The wetness remaining was noticeable to her. Her gaze drifted to Drag's mouth.

"Already thinking about me, I see?"

His cockiness washed away her postcoital glow. She spider-crawled out from between his legs and moved to push herself up.

"You'll be insufferable now."

"Tell me…did my good girl enjoy it?" That look he leveled at her with his blue eyes, possessive and serious, speared her in place.

She pressed her palms hard against the rug beneath her, and she couldn't find the words to speak. She was a wash of joy and happiness and at the same time devastation because she'd missed this. Missed being praised, missed being his. He'd used the word 'my' on top of the 'good girl', phrases she'd heard in dreams for the last twelve years.

She gave a nod.

"Don't answer me with silence. Good girls talk with words."

And she'd be one, damn it, forced to by his phrasing. "I did."

"Excellent. Now, we need to get out of here before those guards come back." He stood and offered a hand to her. She hesitated to take his peace offering, debating continuing to be vulnerable to him. Did she dare to risk more of herself?

He'll hurt me.

In the end, she accepted his hand out of their burgeoning truce. She couldn't dismiss his willingness to give her pleasure even after everything and taking nothing for himself. The temptation to ask him for more was so strong, like a gale-force wind in a nightstorm. She clamped it down, as she did every emotion she had that didn't fuel her push for a future unencumbered by men who would try to control her.

"Yes, let's get out of here. You placed the last one?"

He snapped his fingers. "No, good call."

It took Drag less than five seconds to put the camera in place. By that time, Bridget was already at the door, one hand wrapped around handle. Normally after such a release she'd be ready to relax, sated and spent. Instead, anxiety had mixed with the memories. Not to mention every step she took sent her right back to before with her wet panties a constant reminder of the moment they'd shared.

"Ready?" she asked as he did another cautious look around the room.

"Yeah…this office seems a little more ostentatious than the others, doesn't it? The rich colors of the paint, the desk has a polished rock top. I haven't seen those things."

Bridget forced herself to focus on the room details. Drag was correct, the standard office items from the chairs to the rug were fancier in design or brighter in color than what they'd seen in the other offices, raising the question how the commissioner for Wespero was getting the funds to cover the costs.

"They're definitely not standard… I hate to say it, but this one might be who we're looking for." The connection made sense to her, since Cheatham would have easy access to Paulos.

Drag crossed the room to her, his gaze trailing over her body, and she found herself rocking back and forth on the balls of her feet under his scrutiny. Her skin flushed and she tugged at the sleeves of her shirt.

"Back there…on the floor, we still got it, don't we?"

Had what? Insane levels of sexual attraction?

"We have a connection. Might be because of our past," she replied.

He stepped in close, crowding her until her back came up against the door. "That's it? A little dismissive, because it's not just the past that grants me the knowledge of what will get you damp or make you come. I smell it on you, see it in how your eyes react to me. I sense you, and when I'm close, the tether remains. The same thing connecting me to you all these years. I tried to deny it before, but no lie, it's still there." Drag paused and slapped his cybernetic hand against the door. Nothing broke, thank gods. "Look at me."

She dared to lift her gaze to meet his eyes, even as his words were winding through her like marsanium sludge fuel flooding an engine. She'd overheat at all his confessions and the worst was her heart soared to hear these things, to cling to the possibilities such admissions could create for them.

"We could have had this the whole time between us. Pleasure, satisfaction and hell" — he paused and sighed, glancing up at the ceiling then back down at her — "we make a good team. Look what we did here today."

They did — they always had. Their future had been destroyed by her father and by Cheatham and she'd tried so hard to save what they were supposed to have. Could they get it back?

"Can you tell me why?"

She wanted to. The words were bubbling up, the truth of what had happened. How her father had promised her to someone else and if she killed him… Gods, it would still sound awful but she'd done it all for them. Then Drag had spit in her face and called her a murderer. He'd turned away. If she told him the truth and he abandoned her again… Her throat clenched up, locked in fear.

A knock at the door cut off the opportunity for her to disappoint Drag. But she was sure the guards weren't due back for a couple of solar minutes. They still had time. Drag pushed Bridget to the side, then behind him. She reluctantly let go of the door, her means of escape cut off, though she had a moment's reprieve from the conversation.

Drag opened the door to peek out at their intruder. "What the hell do you want?"

Bridget couldn't see who it was, but Drag's frame had gone rigid, which implied their visitor was someone he knew and didn't want to talk to.

"Where is Bridget? She is missing the opportunity to fulfill her duties."

The dead, even tone of the Trio's voice chilled her to the bone. How the hell had they found her? Did that mean everything they'd done was known to them? Were her plans ruined?

"Why don't you fuck off?"

Drag was prepared to hit first and figure the rest out later. She'd been ready to talk to him, at least he believed so by the way she had hesitated rather than answering straight away. He'd been about to get answers to the biggest question that had plagued him for twelve years. Instead, an agent of destruction had interrupted his plans.

Bridget tugged at his arm as she came around beside him, revealing to the Inccukai she was with Drag. He didn't like her actions at all. He'd been prepared to deny everything.

"We're having a meeting."

The Inccukai's eyes glowed red. "Your *physical discussions* will have to wait. The commissioners grow weary waiting for you."

Bridget's hold on his arm tightened and Drag was starting to see how hard Bridget was trying to remain strong against someone who scared her. "I told you to act in my stead."

"They refused."

"She can verify that...so hope you're not lying," Drag countered. He wanted to tear this sludge sack up. For more than just Bridget. For those of his gang who'd run into this klog in the past. That encounter had left scars and for once Drag wanted to inflict them. That protective nature of his was emerging toward Bridget.

Need to lock that shit up.

Because she'd yet to prove she was worthy, though she had submitted to him so sweetly and come at his damn command. They shared a bond that still existed, at least from a sexual perspective. She might betray him again, but he'd get something out of the deal.

"I attempted and they told me my work wasn't sufficient since I'm hired help and not an official representative of Macintosh. They would only allow me to be present for some of the proceedings. Without your presence, you forfeit Macintosh's place as a backup for Wespero should one of the other gangs have to drop out."

Those words seemed to affect Bridget more. Her frame shook a bit and Drag wanted to know the hidden meaning behind these words. There was more happening than what she'd told him.

Frustration flooded him again, and he straightened his stance, shrugging off Bridget's hold on his forearm. The woman was so locked into whatever implication the Inccukai's words held she didn't appear to notice the distance Drag had created between them.

"Tell them I'll be there shortly. Let me have a few minutes to compose myself."

The Inccukai nodded. "You should fix your hair, too. Gives you too much of a fresh fucked look."

"Watch your damn language." Drag threw the door open the rest of the way and readied his fists.

"Calm yourself, cyborg. We speak out of respect for Macintosh leader. Don't want her to leave a bad impression with the commission or give them reason to alert her sponsor. He wouldn't like you touching what belongs to him." The Inccukai turned and left without preamble. Drag didn't miss how they moved without a sound, even covered head to toe in draping clothes, with white wrappings covering any inch of exposed skin, including the bulk of their face, except for those damn creepy eyes.

Once the assassin was out of sight, Drag put his attention on Bridget. She stood stock still, her eyes a little disoriented and a slight shiver running up and down her body over and over again.

"I'm screwed... It's all over." Her words were a soft whisper.

Drag grabbed her by both arms and turned her to face him. "No, it's just starting. What are you talking about?"

"The Inccukai…they'll tell Cheatham and we won't even be able to combat him. They found out before we could even get underway, and I tried so hard to keep this a secret." She kept going mumbling about how she'd failed, how her life was ruined and she'd be forced to marry Cheatham to give up her future.

Protect her. Ironside's words were on repeat in his head like a Dawning gang meditation chant pounding its way into his brain and forming an insane idea he couldn't believe he was ready to put up on offer.

"No, Bridget. It's going to be okay."

Those words didn't stop her, so he did the one thing he could and silenced her with a brutal kiss. It was a rough mashing of lips. He forced his tongue past her entrance to mingle with hers. There was a moment of shock, hesitation, then she joined in. She wound her arms around his neck and yanked on him, as if pulling him downward would somehow increase the closeness. He accepted her enthusiasm for his touch because that would make this all an easier sell.

You've lost your damn mind.

Snapper was going to kill him, but Drag's rock-hard cock was fully on board if it meant he'd get some playtime too. There were a lot of feelings cascading and rippling through him at the moment. Somehow, he found the wherewithal to slow the kiss and break them apart.

He grinned at her glazed-over eyes, filled with lust and a hint of that blissed-out way she looked after an orgasm. Reaching down, he dipped two fingers between her legs, and ran them right up the seam of her pants, up the apex against her. Her wetness was still present.

"Good girl, you haven't forgotten."

Calling her that name made her let loose a tiny moan. "Why are you doing this?"

"You needed a distraction and what's more, I preferred you not lost in fear, but paying attention to what I have to say…because it's important."

Bridget sighed. "I appreciate you trying to cheer me up, but nothing changes this. The Inccukai will tell Cheatham we're plotting. He'll stop us and that will be that. I lose Macintosh and everything—"

"Stop it. I do have the solution."

"What could possibly salvage this?" She eyed him with skepticism.

Not a surprise she didn't have faith in him. He'd left her, with good reason, but he'd prove himself to her, though he still expected her to bend this situation if it suited her. Even now, her panic showed she was apt to rash decisions if threatened.

"We announce our engagement."

Chapter Nine

"This is a shit idea." Snapper's words were paired with tossing a tire rim the length of the mechanics bay. The sharp screech of metal cutting into metal could be heard as the rim met the bay door.

"Well, shit or not... It's happening." Drag had been surprised when Bridget considered his suggestion a viable option.

She'd been all sorts of happy after that as they proceeded to join the main group and review the schedule of events for the upcoming championship. Drag would be expected to make a couple appearances. The others could be handled by his fellow gang members. He'd need to do a test run to prove the racer was stable. Everyone had to participate, then the placing round of five laps to determine starting order would occur, followed by the opening ceremony and banquet, then the race.

Afterward, he and his crew had returned to Frog Lick and he longed to know if Bridget was regretting her agreement to his proposal. *Engagement? Fuck, I am crazy.*

"I knew this would happen. You get around she-slither and it's like she wraps you up, captures your gaze and brainwashes you into stupid decisions. What did she offer this time? Free roam of her person until this is done?"

Drag clenched his fists as he leaned against the wall. He didn't like how Snapper spoke about her. She didn't deserve that kind of treatment, or at least Drag was aggravated at how dismissive Snapper was of the situation.

"I didn't think of that, but it's beyond the point. There is more to this than me and her. We need to keep the suspicion off of us, at least remove the notion from anyone's brains that we're investigating Cheatham. Nothing implausible about the fact we reconnected after twelve years and discovered the passion is still there."

Snapper stopped his pacing and got in Drag's face. "Is it?"

"Does it fucking matter?" Drag countered.

"It does when you're putting this entire gang on the line. You better be right…if you're all about dipping your dick—"

Drag grabbed Snapper around the throat and gently squeezed. "I don't appreciate you talking about her like that."

Joseph's balls, what am I doing?

He released the hold on Snapper, shame flooding his entire body. They'd fought before, but never with true anger playing into the situation. Their battles dealt in words and held some sort of respect in tone, but this dove right into dirty territory.

His friend let out a hoarse cough as he rubbed his throat. "Never knew a situation where you chose her over me. She would have killed me if you hadn't sided with me before. Now you're willing to let her sacrifice everything we've built."

Drag shook his head. "That's not the case. This is to prevent our beginning efforts from going to ruin. You said yourself, Gina's already collecting information that might prove damning. If Cheatham suspects, he might pull away, but if we make this about Bridget and myself, that changes things."

Snapper swore. "I hate how you're making a bit of sense when it's really bothering me that you're getting involved with my sister again."

"Feeling those familial bonds?" A bad joke to make but Drag wanted this to be less a fight and more a conversation. He had to lighten the mood.

"Ugh." Snapper stuck out his tongue. "More worried about my chosen family than a blood relation that would rather see my corpse burning if it meant ensuring she still had power."

It'd been years since they'd discussed the reality of the situation they were in. How Bridget had claimed leadership over Macintosh, a position that should have gone to Snapper instead.

"It still bothers you?"

Snapper's attention moved to him, those eyes of his burning with regrets. "She killed our father. The man wasn't perfect, hell... He only acknowledged me in secret, but I was supposed to take the mantle. I at least wanted the option to relinquish the claim, not be forced to give up upon threat of death. Still surprised she didn't send an assassin to kill me."

Truer words were never spoken. Drag had expected it over the years. He and Snapper always prepared for thieves in the night, hired would-be killers that never arrived. Bridget had opted to leave them alone.

"Which makes the story more interesting, doesn't it? Ironside said some weird shit to me. This fake engagement will help me get the answers. We need to know when all this is said and done, she's not going to try the same bullshit again. Though I wouldn't have left threats alive if it were me."

Snapper chuckled. "Oh sure, you're too nice, Drag. At the end of the day, you hope there's good in everyone, even Bridget. I think you're going to go looking for reasoning and find the cracked mind of a woman who didn't want to be controlled."

Now that Drag didn't believe. Not for one second, when she submitted to him sexually with little fight. No, she craved the possibility of giving in and he'd give her more opportunities for the same. In that way she hadn't changed. Was it possible she had a good reason for making the choices she had?

"Eh, we'll see. In the meantime, will you attend the announcement ceremony?"

"No." Snapper shook his head. "You won't catch me anywhere near that town. Not after rescuing Jack. I'll stay here and do my job, which is prepare this damn racer for the championship. Take Jack and Shannon. Hell, some of the others. They'll enjoy the escape, and they aren't tainted by what happened to us back then."

Drag wouldn't push for Snapper's participation. His best friend had a point—the racer and their upcoming bid for a possible sponsor of their own were of equal importance to Drag's clandestine work. Dividing and conquering seemed the best route.

Here's hoping I don't screw this up.

* * * *

"My friends, my brothers and sisters. I come before you today to announce that Drag's bid to see if we suit has been successful. We are now engaged." Bridget's announcement from the steps in front of her home sent the gathered crowd into a frenzy of cheers.

There were no frustrated faces or even sneers, to Drag's surprise. He'd been prepared for outrage and malcontent among those of Macintosh, for them to express some sort of objection to their gang allying with another via marriage.

Instead, he was pulled away from Bridget by a group of men. Many of the faces were similar to those he'd grown up with, though they were the looks not of boys, but of men, some more hardened than others.

A mug of brew was stuffed into his human hand. Toasts were made and the men assailed him with thanks for the shared technology and the farming techniques. The appreciation was replicated around the circle with more toasts to future success and allyship.

"You'll be able to truly lead us. Not with that half-hearted work Bridget has done."

Interesting, how the conversation had in quick fashion turned to Bridget and her lack of leadership. Others agreed with the first man.

"But she's helped you keep a sponsor all these years." Hell, twelve years with a single sponsor was almost unheard of without continuous winning.

"That's because Cheatham planned to marry her. Now that you've claimed her suit instead, I'm sure he'll abandon us."

"No problem there, because Drag will win the championship and both Macintosh and Full Throttle can benefit. We have shipbuilding capabilities."

"You're a smart one, Drag. That's why we need you. Who would have thought up such an ingenious plan around the blockade?"

The sentences flying back and forth framed his plan in a whole new light. To outsiders, even Cheatham, Drag would appear to be trying to find a workaround to the shipbuilding ban. The marriage would bring a lot of questions as well. For both gangs.

This could work. Cheatham will think I'm up to something else and not investigating him.

Hell, it might even force the bastard to try some more bribes to deal with him...or deploy the assassin. That made Drag grin as he took another big gulp of his ale. A fight with that bandaged-up idiot would feel damn nice and more of a workout than he'd get in hand-to-hand combat with anyone else.

"Well, I'm glad I have your support."

"You have more than that." This came from one of the older men. "We never felt comfortable with Bridget's takeover. A female in charge of a gang is unheard of."

"That Aurestral gang has a female leader."

"Yeah, but she has a husband."

Around they went again, debating the merits of a female in charge. These people were idiots. They weren't starving, they had challenges with generating water for consumption, but everyone did. With Full Throttle's help, they could get that taken care of.

Their statements about not wanting a female in charge hit Drag wrong as well because not once had they stood up for him and Snapper when Bridget was calling for their heads. No, they had been all too eager to let the fighting carry on, with Drag having to scrap for both their lives. He'd lost his arm and they'd both been cast out with only Rune and Petal to help as they struggled.

Bridget had been the one to start with the taking of Snapper's arm, then she'd finished up the job when Drag had hesitated. Years had passed before he could forgive himself for that hesitation. Snapper's words of frustration could be seen mirrored here in this conversation.

"She was always power-hungry."

"Drag, you had a good reason for killing him, right? He denied your suit the first time?"

"What's past is past, leave the man alone!"

Those memories were even worse, when she'd cut at Snapper's arm then followed with accusing Drag and Snapper of being murderers in return, that they were the ones guilty of the plot. Trying to reverse the accusation back to the real culprit was impossible.

Cheatham had backed Bridget's story. He'd claimed he had seen both Drag and Snapper plan their dastardly coup and take the leader's life. Bridget had acted in retribution. She'd avenged her father's death and for that deserved leadership.

"The old man's right. The past should stay where it belongs, dead and burned beyond recognition. What matters is the amends I'm making now, and how my gang is willing to partner with me and support working with our neighbors and soon-to-be brother-gang." Drag's announcement brought a good amount of cheers and clanking of mugs together as they all finished off their drinks.

"More beer!"

Drag's mug was ripped away, and the small group moved in the other direction. That gave him a chance to look for Bridget. The woman in question, her red hair down and cascading in spiraling waves over her shoulders, with a deep green floor-length dress covering her body while accentuating her breasts, stood not more than three feet behind him.

Her face wasn't angry or filled with happiness, but more impassive and contemplative, her head cocked a bit to the right at an angle. The expression made Drag fearful she'd heard everything. The last thing was for Snapper to be right and the Macintosh members' adoration toward him causing bigger issues or threatening Bridget's sense of seniority.

She walked toward him, looping her arm through his. "I'm not surprised by what they said but still unsure how many of them are just trying to spread ideas on behalf of Cheatham. You handled them well."

"Did I?" Concerning that she believed there to be spies everywhere. "Are you always this distrusting?"

"To the first question, yes. You kept them from getting in a heated debate which could have led to a duel in the ring in the morning. As for the second, I've found in my years since you were banished that trust is too dangerous and always ensures something will be used against me."

Drag stroked his cybernetic fingers along the inside of her forearm, enjoying how he could sense her arousal just from that limited touch. The upgrade of the nanites in his cybernetic system still surprised him in ways he didn't expect.

"Well, I'll agree that most people always want something from a leader, but it doesn't mean they can't be relied upon."

Snaps and sparks to the left made them both jump and Drag chuckled as he realized the noises were from the ignition of the torches to light the bonfire as the sun had already dipped low on the horizon, casting a strange deep orange and light purple glow over everything.

"Seems like you're just as alert and wary as I am."

"Well, I'm in an enemy territory. Can you say that you should feel the same in your home?"

At that moment, the rumble of haulers could be heard. He picked up at least two. Glancing for Jack, he caught the other driver's attention and motioned for reconnaissance. His fellow cybernetic friend took off at a run, dodging between attendees toward the main open road into Macintosh.

"You don't have to do that. I know who's coming," Bridget said. She was the epitome of calm and collected.

"How would you know that? Did you invite them?"

"You did as soon as we got caught in that room together."

"Cheatham?"

She nodded and he noticed how she bit her lip. Her skin had gone a shade paler than before.

"Will you be okay?"

She took a deep breath then angled to look at him. "I'll be fine. Besides, better we get this over with sooner. It will help take the heat off us as we wait to see what Gina finds from the cameras. I guess I'd be a little too optimistic if I hoped you were going to have an update as an engagement present?"

"Oh, princess… Yeah, afraid I can't work miracles."

She straightened her spine and watched as the hauler came into view. "Well, then, let's make the best of this. Excuse me, I'll have to prepare lodging for him."

Then she was gone, moving through the crowd toward a small group of men and women who she started to instruct. He wanted to keep an eye on her but needed to prepare to greet Cheatham. If she lost her nerve now, he wouldn't know until it was too late. But in the meantime, Drag would try to keep her separated from Cheatham unless he was present.

She wasn't the only one who was running around skeptical. No, he was fighting off the fears that he'd be betrayed or that all those who'd toasted him minutes before would steal away their support with a mere word. Maybe being around her was making him worse.

"Well, well…Michelson. It's been a long time since I've seen your face." Moag Cheatham's voice was still smooth as silk fabric, though it tended to make anyone feel dirty when they heard his words directed at them. This charismatic manipulator had to have secured all his money through questionable means. He was somewhat attractive but his eyes were devoid of life, similar to killers Drag had met.

"Not long enough, if you ask me."

The man was a liar and lived up to his name. "Then why the hell are you here trying to steal my woman?"

* * * *

Bridget set to work. Hearing those haulers came as no surprise. She figured Trio had gotten a message off to Cheatham after leaving her and Drag in that room. When her sponsor had landed, he'd been updated by his spies about the engagement announcement.

She had no option but to get his lodging ready and hope their celebration would throw Cheatham off the real work they were doing.

Since she had already dispatched a group to make up the guest home they kept for the sponsor, everything would be fine. She poured herself a glass of whiskey, a bottle she kept hidden for herself. Raising the glass, she took a good swallow.

"Newly engaged and I had to hear it from my hired help. Shame, Bridget."

She spit out the drink to stop herself from choking, then started coughing due to the burn in her throat from the little that had evaded her dispel.

"Oh, do you need help?" He touched her back with his thin clammy hand and she recoiled across the kitchen, to the opposite wall.

"I'm. Fine" – another cough, and she swallowed hard as tears gathered at the edges of her eyes – "Give me a minute. You shouldn't sneak up on people."

"Seems fitting since you tried to sneak things by me. Did you believe I'd accept this sham of an engagement? I told you after this championship race, your rule here ends and you'll marry me as your father originally committed to."

She shrugged. "Drag has a better offer. And as you always say, when you can't beat them, join them. I wasn't having much luck with the traditional ways. An alliance would get us the same benefits."

Cheatham smirked at her. "You're a real piece of conniving work. Your father never could see how much plotting goes on in that little head of yours. But I do. I even admire it, while you constantly try to work against me."

"I don't mean for you to," she retorted.

"You're a bitch that needs to be brought to heel. I breed animals, dogs in particular. We race them on a couple Jupiter moons. Far more exciting than what happens here. Think of what kind of life you'll have enacting your little plans on Callisto, turned toward pursuits that will make me far more crinkle than the scraping of flash that happens here."

The glass was in her hand, and small flick of her wrist would toss the contents on him. She wanted to. How she longed to show him that he'd have to kill her before she'd consent.

"And Macintosh?"

"You don't agree, and I'll burn this damn town and its gang to the ground. It's simple, Bridget. You know how the game is played and you hold no cards. You already went all in, as they say at the gambling tables."

She shook her head. "No, I haven't. You said if I won the race."

"But you won't." He took a step closer, and she dreaded his slimy body anywhere near her. He was muscular, but still lithe and with an easy four inches of height on her. She hated looking up at him.

"Doesn't it count if I'm married to the racer that wins?"

"A loophole, nice try. You marry him and I'll kill him."

"You wanted their racer plans, their technology… This is my way in and you're already trying to stifle it because of some jealousy. I thought you played a long game better than that?"

She had no choice but to summon the bravado. Hard as hell when she had started to enjoy the moments with Drag where she wasn't always putting up her guard. She needed to remember that the freedom to be herself wasn't a reality and might never be.

"Long…more like a century game. I'll pass an entire lifetime in the amount of time it takes you to get something done. And I'm not jealous of anything, least of all a man who has one arm." Cheatham took another step toward her right as she saw the main door curtain sweep aside.

"You should be, Moag. I've killed men with this here replacement arm. Don't believe me? You can ask the crowd outside."

Bridget's heart soared as Drag entered her home. The idea of him coming to her defense seemed near impossible. She'd expected Cheatham to make his move while Drag was busy interacting with those of Macintosh. She'd never planned on him pulling himself away from the crowd to check on her.

Instead, here he was right within her doorstep, cracking his knuckles and ready to impart violence on her behalf.

"This doesn't concern you, Michelson. Don't interfere. A sponsor has a right to discuss misgivings with their gang leader."

"And it appears as if she already told you how this is going down. She went all in the minute she decided to come back to me."

What the hell is he saying? Had he heard everything? She hoped not, because those were lies. She'd spoken bullshit with the goal of getting this bastard to let her move forward.

Cheatham laughed, the smooth cadence another mesmeric trick to make people believe he possessed emotion. "You know she'll betray you as soon as someone else offers her a better deal, right? Might as well cut your losses now."

"The only thing I'm going to cut is you, if you don't back off and leave her alone."

Her sponsor looked at Drag with absolute contempt, then spat in his direction. The fluid landed on her floor about halfway to Drag. "Men have died for less. They don't dare to challenge me."

"Well, I do."

Was this even real life? Drag standing up to Cheatham? She'd dreamed of this one too many times and always woke up to the nightmare that was her life without fail. Now Drag stood here ready to throw down without prompting.

"You're a true bastard. Not worthy of leadership."

Drag shrugged as he started to move toward her. "Not the first time someone's accused me of such and won't be the last. You'll need to come up with better insults if you want them to land, Moag."

"I'm still the sponsor here."

Bridget tried to keep her smile under control, face impassive, even though she wanted to squeal at seeing Cheatham reduced to so few words. This had to be a record for the man who never wanted to stop talking. Him barely managing a good comeback filled her with delight.

"Yeah, you're a sponsor." Drag reached her and wrapped an arm around her shoulders. She couldn't help but sink into his embrace. With his other hand he took the whiskey glass from her and downed the rest of the drink. "That's why she prepared your quarters. Kicked a family out of their home for the evening. I'd say you'd do best retiring for the night. Maybe work that sponsorship part with your usual tours of the shipyard, the mines, the mechanic bay and the new airponics setup Full Throttle has helped with. See your benevolence at good work."

"Is that a threat?" Cheatham had stopped his forward advancement, but his brain was obviously already trying to find a workaround.

"No. I don't waste time with threats. If you're expecting something from me, be sure I'll act before I speak. I just figured you'd want to reassure the good people of Macintosh how happy you are with their work and how this alliance will be benefiting everyone."

Cheatham's gaze darted between them, and Bridget was as solemn faced as she could manage. Inside she was a ball of excitement, ready to explode, like a racer revved up at a starting line. If Cheatham didn't leave soon, she might ruin the moment with her laughter.

"That's your cue to exit." Drag motioned toward the front door.

When Cheatham started to move, Drag followed, and Bridget was left without his warm body to support her. She wobbled a bit then stood straight. The fact she let Drag step in was as foreign as him being here. A world of firsts, when she typically had to fight her own battles.

She watched the pair, opposing foes in both manners and looks. The graceful Cheatham in his flowing robes and Drag who was pure bulky muscle and wearing his usual boots, pants and simple shirt getup. Nothing fancy, but the gleam of his cybernetic arm would ensure no one questioned what he chose to wear.

They were also similar in height, but from there the differences were more striking. Drag's very presence commanded attention whereas she would've overlooked Cheatham in a crowd. The one thing that bastard had going for him was his ability to trap people in horrible situations and take away their means of escape.

Not this time.

Cheatham stopped for a brief moment at the entrance, flashing a scathing look at Drag and mumbling about the outrage of being treated so poorly, then the bastard left. Drag took something out of his pocket and placed it beside the door frame. The little black square stuck, and with a press of a button, an electric field covered the entire door with a spark and shimmer.

"What's that?"

Drag turned around and started to work his way back toward her, with a wicked grin on his face. "Protection, something you've been lacking."

"How do I control it?"

"Better question is what are you going to do for me now that I've gotten rid of that sludge sack?"

Not hard to tell what Drag wanted her to do, or at least she could tell he was seeking something physical by the graceful and sleek way he approached. Like a coon cat hunting a goosemert, slow, methodical stalking of a prey, though she wasn't a flight risk. The last time they'd been together had left her craving more for days.

"What do you want?"

"Strip and I'll show you."

Chapter Ten

Drag had been told from a young age that he had a problem.

"You always push for more..." Words imparted from his mother. His uncle had laughed and exclaimed Drag had nuggets of steel for going after what he wanted. But he didn't know another way to be.

When Drag found himself with the advantage, why not ask. The worst anyone said was no, but most people were so shocked he dared to try in the first place, they would give him what he wanted. This approach worked with women, men, trading...any situation he found could easily be approached with driving toward his goals and seeing how often people would reciprocate.

With Bridget right now, she was no different. She could say no, but he believed she'd give in.

He'd sensed her excitement when he had arrived and taken control of the situation. *Rather shocked she let me.* Bridget preferred to fight her own battles without hesitation. Someone stepping in wasn't looked upon with kindness. Even when they had been kids, she'd attack someone before letting him step in and take care of it. Another reason those jackasses talking down about her were wrong. She wasn't afraid to put herself in the first line of fire.

"I just drop the dress?" she asked, cocking her head to the side and lowering the fabric over one shoulder.

"Keep going." He wanted to see all of her. How had her body changed in the years they'd been apart? Did she still have that cluster of freckles on the right side of her belly?

This was the conclusion they had been driving to the moment he'd stepped foot in this house. Moag had been dismissive to him outside at the party, chiding him for attempting to regain Bridget's favor. The sponsor seemed to imply that his goodwill toward Bridget and Macintosh granted him the ability to lay claim to her.

Then a group of men had come over to greet them, the same idiots from before and a whole new addition of fools. Drinks were shared and Moag had snuck off, only for Drag to find him threatening Bridget.

He'd been close to tearing the room apart and ripping Moag's limbs from his body but had found a way through the red haze of rage to use communication to remove the sludge sack from the house. With his adrenaline still pumping, he was filled with this desperate need to prove to himself she'd have him. Especially the new him.

Orgasms fueled by danger and excitement were one thing. This was something else…an impulsive urge to have her. To prove that what had happened a couple days prior wasn't a fluke. The one way would be to challenge her to join him. To submit.

The dress came off the other shoulder, and she slipped her arms out of the loops that functioned as barely-there sleeves. The green fabric was held up by her breasts now, the creamy tops just visible.

He bit his lip and took a step closer before pausing. A game of give and take, but she wouldn't get him without letting go, exposing herself.

She winked, always the tease, then tugged at the bodice, uncovering her breasts. Her flesh so pale compared to the tan of her face and arms, but he was more mesmerized by the pink hue to her hardened nipples and the piercings that went through each one.

"Those are new," he couldn't help remarking.

"Do you like them?"

No comment at this point—how he could he tell without getting closer?—which he refused to do until she was naked.

"You'll find out as soon as that dress is gone."

She tugged once more, then shimmied her hips and the whole confection of green fell to the floor, pooling at her booted feet.

"Good girl," he said, loving how she shivered under his praise. "Step out of those boots, too."

"I might fall. This dress is slippery."

He was at her side in four steps, then picked her up in his arms. There was something glorious about holding a naked woman, and even more that it was this particular woman. "Get rid of them."

Each boot clunked to the floor, her feet so damn dainty she could just slip out of them. Though he wondered. "Why aren't your boots fit to size?"

She glanced at him, then away, her hesitation worrisome. Finally, she said, "I refused to get boots unless the entire town would be fitted."

The answer stunned him a bit and was in juxtaposition with how he'd expected her to behave after he left. She'd always been big about fancy things and wanting items or clothing far more expensive than others had.

"Truth?"

"I'm a leader. If I walked around in the newest fashions and offers just because my sponsor would grant them to me, how fast would the entire gang resent me?"

A valid reasoning, and one he'd mentioned to those who partnered with him over and over. How the hell could such a confession make him more aroused? But it did. If she was lying, she seemed to know the exact words that would make him a sucker for her.

"That's such good behavior. All your sacrifices deserve rewarding, and I think I know just what to do."

She clung to him tighter as he started to move.

"Which way, princess?"

She pointed toward the small hallway opposite from her father's room. "My bedroom. Hasn't changed."

"You didn't move into the main room?"

The past loomed heavy again—how could any of this interaction not include it? Instead of responding, she pulled on his neck and he bowed his head to accept her kiss, the mere meeting of lips so brief but filled with plenty of longing. His heart hammered in his chest.

"I refused to leave behind the place that gave me a part of you."

Fuck. He marched, steps sure and quick even as his cock strained against his pants. He'd make her orgasm so many damn times she'd never want to leave the room again. The room itself looked the same. A press of a button and the heating coil came to life, along with a small light near her bedside.

There were the drawings, pictures she'd put together. The map of the territories along her wall. The closet burgeoning with her clothes, and the wide rug in the center. Her bed, large enough for the both of them, against the far wall. He was tempted to toss her onto it, but opted to give her more worship versus how he'd treated other partners in their time apart.

A well-earned reward, since she submitted so beautifully and was answering his questions without reservation. As he laid her on the bed, letting her sink onto the softness of the comforter, she opened her mouth then shut it again.

"Speak, princess. You want something, you know how good girls get what they want. Ask."

Bridget trailed a hand over his cheek. "I want your cock, and I don't want to wait."

"Where?"

She winked in return. "Pick a hole and take me."

He growled at her offering. The way she gave herself to him without any hesitation strained his tenuous hold on his control. Even though he wasn't quite a whole human anymore, he wasn't fazed. Shucking his shirt, he watched her writhe in excitement on the bed.

"Ready yourself for me, but I want to watch." He grabbed one of her feet and turned her body so he could get a good look at her pussy. It was already glistening from arousal.

I caused that.

How he turned her on puffed him up a bit. He couldn't help but admire his own effect on her and he'd just gotten started.

"Be good and play with that pussy."

She reciprocated by dipping two fingers in between her lips, spreading them wide to take a couple fingers from her other hand. He had a good view as he continued to divest himself of his remaining clothing.

Once naked, he stroked his cock, rubbing the precum over his head and allowing himself to enjoy the show Bridget was putting on. Her red locks were a fan of fire across the mattress, her skin flushed from her exertion as she worked to get herself off.

"You're so beautiful, spread wide for me and touching yourself. Do you think you should come without me?"

She shook her head and continued her fingering.

"Those aren't words. Answer or I'll be jerking off all over your tits instead of stuffing you with this cock."

"No, I don't want to come without you."

He stepped forward, rubbing the head of his cock over her fingers and clit. "Then clear the way."

She was slick, hot and eager as she flexed her hips, trying to catch his dick. But he held himself still for a moment, enjoying her desperation and also mentally preparing himself.

Being with her after so long, there was this deep-seated longing crawling upward from the abyss he'd locked it in. The hope this wouldn't be the last time he'd get to have her. Sex hadn't been the same with others. Those were quick romps, meant to satisfy an urge, but nothing like the connection he'd shared with her.

He reached out and put a hand to her waist, stilling her movements. No, this would be irrevocable. As much as he might try to ruin her for all others, she would do the same to him, no doubt. There was an opportunity here to stop, but no way could he walk away from this now.

He slid in nice and slow, enjoying how she absorbed every inch of his cock, filling her up and reveling in how damn tight she was, so fucking turned on that her pussy walls were like the sweetest clamp he'd ever experienced.

Then she licked her lips and begged, "Please move."

"Can't deny you, since you asked nice-like." So, he moved, stroke by stroke, a steady pace that sent a pleasurable tingle through his entire body.

Though not enough as Bridget started to play with her nipples, tweaking those little bars between them. *Shit, I need to give them attention as well.*

Keeping his pace, he leaned over and sucked one into his mouth. Bridget moaned, her usual quiet panting morphing into something new. He kept repeating the motions and trying new ones, flicking the bar, twisting it with his tongue, biting her flesh and seeing what combinations produced the sweet music of sexual gratification from her mouth.

Her first orgasm hit then, as her back arched and she let out a low wail that ended in, "Fuck. More. Please."

Increasing his pace, he worked his mouth up her throat and last to her lips, swallowing her screams of pleasure as his cybernetic nanite speed took over. The upgrade allowed him to accelerate his movements faster than a regular human. He kissed Bridget with desperation and the hope this wasn't just a one-off situation.

This was what he'd missed on the lonely nights — her surrounding him. Her scent of citrus and leather that still clung to her skin. The way her nails, even these short ones, bit into his biceps and how her tongue danced with his. Her body stilled as another orgasm began to crest and he found himself joining her in release, but he wouldn't spill inside of her.

No, he pulled out and let his seed spray across her belly, the sticky slick hitting his chest as well. There were no guarantees of a pregnancy on Mars, but the risk was higher in Macintosh. Their antiquated attitudes toward women meant they didn't partake in the medical clinics that offered women a chance to control their fertility.

He moved to pull away so he could clean her up but she held him tight to him, refusing to let him move. "Bridget, let me fix this mess."

"No, don't let it end yet. Hold me." She encouraged him to lay over her, pressing her down with his weight.

"I don't want to hurt you."

"Compared to what's already happened, you couldn't hurt me any worse than I hurt myself."

The words lodged in his chest, so he spooned in beside her and held her close until she fell asleep.

* * * *

Bridget startled awake at the feel of a warm cloth on her belly. Drag was there cleaning up his semen from their romp earlier in the evening. Hell, it was still dark.

"What time is it?"

"Pretty early in the morning, before sunrise." Drag kept his attention on her stomach as he cleaned. "You still have the freckles."

He pressed a kiss to the little cluster above her hip and her chest got tight. There were so many memories of him with her in this bed. The sexual desire they shared was something that hadn't seemed to wane over the years. The way he treated her body with reverence and at the same time possessed the recollection of what to do to make her orgasm without difficulty... He was different in some ways, but still the same.

"Why don't you touch me again? This time with your mouth?"

Drag lifted his head and grinned. "Is that a request or a demand?"

"Do you care if it's both?" Now that she'd let her mind wander to the idea, her body was waking up. His hands on her shot tendrils of arousal through every nerve. She wanted more than his warm heat, but in the place she'd gone too long without oral attention.

"I may have to take my words from earlier back. You're not just good, you're very, very dirty," he said.

It was her turn to smile as she put her hands on either side of his head, moving him to where she wanted his mouth. "You wouldn't like me any other way."

He blew a hot breath of air over her core, then dipped his tongue between her lips. She gasped at the penetrative motion, how hot his tongue was and she needed more.

"Don't stop, please."

"What would you give for this?"

"Anything." She was that desperate as he rotated his body and lay down between her legs like a supplicant ready to provide prayers and worship to his deity. *My pussy.*

"Then when I'm done, you're telling me what has happened since I left. I want details. Including why there isn't more success here in Macintosh since you got a sponsor."

A hint of dread started to permeate the edges of her desire, but it was sent hurtling away as Drag began to eat her out. She was the banquet and he the starving man who was determined to devour her. Devour he did and this was as good as his cock filling her. Earlier she couldn't get as close as she wanted to him, during that last leg where he had pounded into her with a speed she'd never experienced.

As a man, he'd always known how to pleasure her, but as a cyborg, he took that ability to new heights. Not to mention how he praised her. When he'd held her while she slept, he had whispered about how good she was. How perfect her body. How he hadn't experienced such a release since they'd parted. The words had calmed her and now the reminder had tears gathering in the corner of her eyes.

He kept working his tongue against her clit, then adding two of his cybernetic fingers, inserting them slowly into her pussy. She tightened the walls and allowed herself to experience the warmth that emanated from them. The sensation spread and soon she was sobbing and shaking as an orgasm hit, then another. A third one joined them and Drag removed his fingers, lapping up her release.

She shivered, but he was there, gathering her into his arms, holding her close. Her tears were still seeping out even as she tried to stop them.

"It's okay. I'm sorry if that was too much." Drag stroked her hair and cradled her in his arms, as if she belonged there. When…she didn't.

"No. It was amazing and more than I deserved." Guilt had overtaken the satisfaction still racking her body. She'd agreed to this knowing that he would always give far more than she should have. "You should hate me and instead you're trying to treat me right. It's not fair. I deserve to be punished."

"Good girls think that way, but you've been through a lot."

She shivered, before sniffling against his chest and whispering, "I'm a murderer."

He stilled his motions and she prepared for the rejection. He'd shove her away like he should, call her names and storm out. She'd lied for years, never confessing the truth, until now, when she couldn't help herself.

Instead, he pressed a kiss to her forehead. "I'm just as much of a killer as you are. We all have choices we have to make for survival. That's living on Mars."

"But I could have chosen differently..."

Could I? Would not killing my father have made a difference? In some ways at least...Snapper and Drag would have been whole. She might not have gotten the life she wanted, but she hadn't when she had chosen the other way, either. So, did it matter?

"Tell me what happened." The words were warm breath against her forehead as he spoke.

She'd promised anything when he brought her to satisfaction, but she wasn't ready to tell him this. Not yet. "I can't. But I will."

Chapter Eleven

Drag poured the hot tea into the cups. He'd brewed it from the supplies Bridget had in the kitchen. After she had passed out again, the sex and her crying session a perfect recipe for exhaustion, Drag had been unable to sleep.

He'd thought they were working toward a truce where she would open up to him, especially when the tears had started. But instead, she'd locked herself up again. Could he have pushed the issue? Sure, but it wouldn't make her talk to him later. They were bound together now by this push to rid Macintosh of Moag.

Whatever had happened back then and leading up to now had left Bridget with scars. Seeing it up close…he was sympathetic toward her in a way that might come back to bite him, though he believed in second chances. He'd been given one when he'd taken over as the leader of Full Throttle. The way to see if this would work was to spend more time with her.

He took the steaming mugs into the bedroom and stood there for a moment, looking down at her sleeping. Her hair was her most definitive feature, though he didn't miss the tan lines on her skin, how her freckles had multiplied in quantity in the areas exposed. The rest of her was creamy, silky flesh. There were bruises on her legs and he could tell she wasn't eating as much.

How they had a sponsor and not enough food didn't make sense. Not to mention the dark color under her eyes implying she hadn't been sleeping well. There were signs of aging too, but those made her more beautiful. Seeing beyond the events that caused him pain allowed him to appreciate how she'd matured into a beautiful woman, though the Macintosh mark on her arm looked different than the one he'd once sported. Leaning in for a closer look, he noticed the indentation of the letter B in the lower half.

Of course, she had to leave her own mark on everyone.

His closeness seemed to work as a wakeup call. She started to stretch and blink her eyes. When she opened them, there was a momentary smile on her face, and he met hers with one of his own, though it disappeared fast. She immediately grabbed for a sheet to cover up the exposed parts of her body.

Shame.

"What are you still doing here?" she asked.

He extended the mug of tea toward her. "Made you something to drink. Breakfast blend I think it is, the one that Restia still makes from the smell of the leaves."

"Okay…still doesn't explain why you're here?" She pushed herself upright and took the mug, blowing over the top of it and eyeing him.

"So, you expected me to sneak out and pretend last night didn't happen?"

"No, I'm just not used to those who see to my needs sticking around."

He sat on the edge of the bed and took a long gulp of the tea, enjoying the burn of the hot beverage as it scorched his throat. He needed it to avoid asking who the hell was pleasuring her and if they held a heating coil to what he'd provided last night.

"How about you get used to it? We're engaged, no one is going to expect any different. In fact, they would be suspicious if they didn't see me spending the night here."

And he would be damned if she wanted to treat these intimate relations as some dirty secret. As far as he was concerned, they were together in all the ways that counted until their mission was resolved. If sex played into it, well then…he was more than down for the fun times. They were electric together in the bedroom and she had never minded his more dominant nature to have control over things.

"All right," she said before she took a sip of the tea. "No raising red flags. Then what's next? You still haven't told me if Gina found anything."

He finished his drink and set down the mug. "How about you come with me to Frog Lick and we find out together? Anyone asks, it's a supply and technology sharing visit. We're supposed to be bringing Macintosh into the future with us."

"And you think she'll have something?"

"No clue…but it will get you away from Moag for a day."

Bridget chuckled, tucking her mug up near her mouth. "You never call him by his surname."

"That implies respect and I have none, not for that space hole who hasn't even ensured the town is well maintained in the last twelve years. The only ones being supported are the miners, ship builders and the mechanics bay. Everything else lacks and you'd all starve without his monthly shipments. That's not the way it should be."

There was more he wanted to say, but his shoulders were tense and getting angry didn't benefit anyone at this moment. All it did was make him second guess why Frog Lick and Full Throttle needed a sponsor. If they were offering what Moag had, then there was no point.

"You're right. He's made us dependent on him to the point if he were to declare me unfit to be in charge, the people would accept his decisions because to risk losing his position as our benefactor would be devastating. He acts like we don't make him the flash, but I know for a fact we make him a ton." She took a sip of her drink, the frown on her face creating a divot in between her eyebrows.

Adorable. And he wanted to fix whatever did that to her to begin with. "Then even better to escape for the day. Come with and we'll see if there's a way to get him out of your life yet."

"I guess I can't say no."

"Not today."

* * * *

They drove into Frog Lick with Bridget sitting up front across from Jack. Drag opted to take the backseat. No denying the experience was strange. He would have never predicted sleeping with Bridget a few weeks ago, let alone riding in a hauler together.

The event was surreal, and played havoc on his senses, reconciling the woman he'd believed her to be and the one he was slowly getting to know again. Though he still hated how she kept things from him.

They pulled to a stop in front of the Watering Hole and Drag hopped out, giving Bridget a hand.

"Thank you," she murmured as they stood there for a minute while Jack turned everything off and climbed out.

Jack had been silent for most of the ride, but then again he didn't have a lot of good feelings toward Bridget. She'd cut off his pinky and beaten the shit out of him. Not to mention she had sicced her assassin on Jack's girlfriend, Shannon.

"Are they all inside?" Drag asked.

"Back room, just like you told me." Jack walked ahead of them and entered the building, but Drag had to wait as Bridget hesitated.

"What's wrong?" he asked.

"I don't belong here. I've hurt everyone that's going to be in that room. They hate me."

He brushed her cheek with the edge of his fingers. "When the hell has what other people thought about you stopped you?"

She shrugged. "Regardless of what you think of me, I'm not as strong as I appear."

He leaned in and pressed a kiss to her forehead, above the sun goggles. "I think you're one of the strongest people I know."

"You say that, but—"

"But you're Bridget fucking Macintosh." The epithet was one he'd taught her to say every time she got nervous or scared. To summon that inner beast of hers and a light a fire that couldn't be squashed no matter what.

She smiled at him, though with the goggles in place he couldn't quite see if it made it to her eyes. "You're right, I am. Let's go."

Fingers crossed those words were enough to get her to brave this slither den. Because no doubt most of his family wouldn't have kind things to say to her. Though he'd already told them she was coming today, he wasn't sure how to approach being around her. Display closeness or shy away? Here he was walking in with nerves and anxious energy flowing through him, his body like an engine about to be overloaded with NiteOx.

I said no secrets, stick to your word.

Determined to be honest as he always was, he wrapped an arm around her shoulder as they entered the gathering spot. It had been a bar, but once he'd taken over in Frog Lick, it had become so much more. Now the Watering Hole was where the gang came together, where meetings were held, where those who were hungry could always go for a bite to eat without paying. Three meals a day to everyone in town, regardless of if they were gang members. Where booze and other libations could be enjoyed. Finally, where music could always be shared.

Entering now with a woman who'd been labeled a sworn enemy mere months before in his arms elicited several questionable gazes, including one from Gaia, though she added a smirk. There was an element of 'told ya so' in her eyes and he'd be hearing something from her later, no doubt.

No one approached them as they crossed the footprint of the main floor and headed down the hallway that led to the back—the unofficial meeting room for all Full Throttle founding members, and those who needed a private audience with Drag or Gaia from time-to-time. The door opened before they reached it, Rune sticking his head out.

"Oh, good. A couple of us were worried you might have trouble." Rune stepped back, pulling the door open the rest of the way. He appreciated his brother for trying to keep the peace. The younger Michelson always believed in solving things without violence. *Probably why he's a better farmer than driver.*

"No issues out in the main room. Are we walking into a nightmare in here?" Drag asked with a chuckle.

Rune didn't answer, which implied they might have issues…most likely from Snapper. Drag would have to deal with his best friend, get him to see that Bridget wasn't as bad as he kept wanting to make her out to be.

"We've arrived," he announced as he crossed the threshold with Bridget tensing up beside him. She was seconds from throwing his arm off, and he opted to rest his weight a bit more on her so she couldn't remove him with ease.

"Good, sure Rune mentioned we were worried," Hemi replied as he stood up. The others were in varying poses from sitting in chairs to staring into the unlit burn pit.

No one could miss Snapper facing away from the main group, his wife's hands on his cheeks, whispering something to him. Gina was obscured and the woman had learned how to lower her voice to a decibel only Snapper could hear.

"Yeah, no riots. We're fine. Anxious to see if Gina has learned anything?" Drag asked.

Snapper turned to him then and pointed at the door. "I need to talk to you."

The tension in the room was back, thick as ever. Bridget gripped his shirt with her fist as Snapper approached them.

He glanced at her. "Don't worry, I'm not going to beat his ass. I'll save that for you, when you fucking hurt him again."

Drag hugged her close and whispered, "Don't worry. I'll be right back. Lead the way, Snap."

He followed his friend out of the room, Jack close on their heels. They walked all the way out of the building and across the road to the mechanics bay. *A long fucking way for a conversation.* Neither Jack nor Snapper said a word, but Drag couldn't help himself.

"Are you playing mediator?"

"Someone may have to, might as well be me."

They all filed into the mechanics bay, which was empty for the day.

"Where is everyone?" Drag asked.

"Gave them the day off, in case you decide that woman needs to come in here. Don't want to continue fueling any speculation about what happens next."

"What happens is we share what Gina found and figure out the next steps. She'll work with Rune and Petal on some more tech pieces of the hydroponics plant and the airponics start-up for Bridget to take back with her."

Snapper sighed. "Why are you doing this, Drag? Jeopardizing everything? I know what you're going say...enemies close and that sort of thing, but tell me the truth. I'm your friend and I deserve to know if you're going to throw Frog Lick over for a nice piece of ass."

Drag flexed his fists, then rolled his shoulders and cracked his neck…everything to keep the anger at bay because it was rising. Instead of directing it at Snapper, he'd hold it in reserve for that bastard Moag.

"Our people, the ones that cast us out, they are suffering under Moag. That sponsorship is a lesson in absolute control and domination. They are starving over there, and without medical necessities."

Snapper shrugged. "Not our problem. That's Bridget's problem the day she decided to kill our father, frame you for the murder and take both our arms. She cut me, would have killed me."

"And I don't know if she had a choice, Snap." Of course, that was a hunch, but all Drag had was this niggling idea that maybe Bridget hadn't wanted to hurt them.

"Your dick is doing the thinking again," Jack chimed in. "I know you didn't leave her place last night. So, tell us the truth, you fucking her?"

A part of him wanted to reply that it wasn't their business, not when what happened in the bedroom should remain private between him and Bridget. Except he wasn't responsible for just one person…he answered to an entire gang.

"Yes, I am. But you two aren't the best people to be casting judgment here."

Jack swore. "Yeah, but my woman considered betraying us — she refrained from doing it."

True, Bridget's crimes against the founding members of Full Throttle were pretty lengthy. "*She deserves a second chance. Protect her.*" Those damn words of Ironside refused to go away.

Snapper snorted. "Gina sought me out. I tried to fight that."

Whatever makes them think better of themselves at the end of the day.

"The bottom line is none of us are perfect," Drag said, giving a shrug. "And she isn't either. All I'm asking for is an opportunity to see where this goes. The ultimate end goal is we get the proof that Moag interfered with our reinstatement for our shipbuilding license. That's all that matters."

Snapper bowed his head then punched a wall. "Fine, I'll follow your lead. Damn it if it's not tearing me up inside, though. Are you prepared for the fact this may not turn out the way you think?"

Am I?

Ever since his gut instinct had been tested twelve years prior, he'd worked hard to trust himself again. Where he believed that he'd been fooled by Bridget, them working together was already making him question those ideas he so firmly held to.

"It probably won't, but it's rare for things to work out the way we expect them to."

"If you have to, will you choose Full Throttle over her?" Jack asked.

This question hit as hard as the other one, a square pounding to his solar plexus, invisible yet as impactful. Where he could philosophize about the other, this one was more straightforward. He went with the first response that sprang to his lips. "Yes, always. Now, can we get back to the others? I'd like to hear Gina's update too."

"No need," Snapper replied right as the mechanics bay door opened. "They were coming here anyway. Easier for Gina to show things direct on the big holoscreen versus a smaller version. Pretty interesting stuff."

Gina walked in, followed by Bridget, then Hemi and Rune. The whole team was together, and he hoped Bridget didn't feel ganged up on. Something was wrong since her polite grin was matched with tension around her eyes.

"Just follow me and ignore those three. They're arguing again, and I hope they don't wreck anything." Gina's words were delivered with plenty of side-eye. For being an AI and only possessing emotions for a short time, she'd been adapting a little too quick to the sarcasm.

Snapper snorted. "What are you trying to imply?"

"You all make too many damn messes," Gina offered right before she pushed open the door to the room that Snapper had cleared for her. Inside she'd become a technological god, giving them access to things they shouldn't have.

For the first time since he'd taken over at Frog Lick, Drag wanted to be anyone but the guy in charge. The longing hit so hard he was shocked by the force of it. But for that brief moment, he wanted to be a regular guy, able to be with a woman without his involvement impacting everyone around him. He wanted Bridget to be a woman unencumbered by expectations. Except that was a fantasy, right? A make-believe world that couldn't exist when they'd fought to become leaders. He had to shovel those rebellious ideas down and accept the destiny he'd made for himself, as well as the one she was seeking with or without him.

My actions impact us all.

The realization was like the shock of being passed on up on the racetrack and watching a win disappear.

It hurt almost as bad as the other revelations he'd been experiencing since arriving in town.

"Hope Gina has things locked up and isn't showing Bridget anything that could hurt us," he murmured as both women disappeared into the room.

"Now you're worried about that?" Jack asked.

"At least we know he's got his big head thinking again," Snapper added.

Drag pushed past both of them with half-hearted shoves and made his way to the room. "Let's get this over with, and you can give me more shit later."

Time to get his head back in the game.

* * * *

Bridget kept her thumbs tucked into her pants pockets to rub the sweat from her palms onto the cloth. She was here in the mechanics bay of the gang she'd considered her sworn enemy since the moment Drag had taken over leadership a few years prior, standing not more than a couple yards from the very racer she'd wanted to get her hands on, and all she could think about were the damn words Drag had uttered. Words she should've never been able to hear, but she'd been unable to resist the temptation to listen in to what was being said, and had slipped a damn listener into his pocket when she'd clung to him in the room at the Watering Hole.

Wasn't difficult to sneak an earpiece in after that, and she'd heard everything on their way over. They'd given the men a couple minute head start before making their way to the mechanics bay, Gina using some excuse that Snapper and Jack needed to address some concerns with the racer.

All bullshit.

No, instead they'd read Drag the riot act, calling her out for being as awful as she already knew she was. For a brief moment, she'd held out hope that Drag was really seeing her without seeing her. He'd even mentioned he didn't believe she'd made her choices for the same lies they'd been spreading all these years.

Then the pivotal question — would he choose her or Full Throttle? That was the first knock against her silly heart. Then another when he was concerned about what she'd see inside this room. How many more times would she continue on this wild path before opting for a backup plan?

Wait until you see what Gina knows.

With holo-screens on three of four walls and a table that could project images, it was a shock how Full Throttle had come into possession of so much tech when they had no flash and no sponsor.

No wonder Drag was wary of letting me in.

She could report them to either commission and have an entire protectorate guard with investigators on site within a day. Their setup implied stealing or illegal dealings. The very optional out she was looking for. *No, I'm not going to betray him again.* She could show with her actions she wouldn't do such a thing.

"Let's get to it then. What have you found?" She needed to direct her focus away from the paranoid anxiety gathering in her mind before she did something rash.

Gina flipped a switch and a holo-vid erupted from the table before her. There were two people in the vid, Cheatham and the Wespero commission member, Paulos.

"These two, no matter how we wished otherwise, are involved in some scheme," Gina said as she started to twist a pair of dials in front of her that both sped up the interaction and zoomed in. "The Macintosh sponsor is paying our elected commissioner off, but for what…"

Gina adjusted another dial and both men could be heard speaking.

"*I trust all is in place.*"

"*Yes, the documents have been drafted, though we have to show probable cause in order to transfer ownership of a gang-town from the current leader. It would have to be severe.*"

Cheatham frowned. "*We already proved cause with that upstart Michelson and the Frog Lick weaklings. Shouldn't be too hard.*"

"*Regardless, I've got everything under lock and key at the shipping commission office. Until we have the additional documentation prepared, we will need witnesses.*"

Gina muted them again as the two started to chuckle and laugh. The idiots thought they were so smart, even as cameras were revealing everything they planned.

"Looks like Moag made an extra stop before heading into Macintosh then," Drag said.

"Yes, and they showed exactly where we can find proof of the sponsor's misdealing, though I imagine they might move the documents ahead of the race. We'll have to move fast, and I've already pulled up the floorplans for the Mars Shipping Commission office."

The holo-vid disappeared, replaced by a three-dimensional image of the building and all the inner workings. It was like magic. While Bridget had heard such technology was available, it had never been something the gangs of Mars possessed, in any territory. This type of capability could make a gang invincible.

Not for the second time today had she contemplated renewing the war just for a chance at the technology within this room. She could have a beating pulse on everything happening on Mars and beyond. To possess the information to cripple any threat or slay a foe before they could react... *Heady shit.*

She didn't miss Drag's pointed look as Snapper took over speaking.

"We've got guard layouts, too. Our best bet is to infiltrate at night, as guard duty is light seeing as the commissioners themselves are not using the main building as frequent right now. The guards' focus is on the vault that controls all the contracts and stores of flash that Mars has from lucrative contracts with the APU government."

"How do you know all this?" Bridget couldn't help asking. The sentences Snapper were uttering seemed impossible.

She continued. "The commission doesn't have flash on hand. That would be impossible when the gangs are the ones allowed to place bets and gain sponsorships."

Snapper opened his mouth to respond, his face full of arrogance with that ridiculous smile as if she was an idiot, but Drag cut him off.

"You were right with what you said before. How members of the commission have gotten comfortable in their roles. They've been subverting the very laws they've upheld for years. Those who get a chance to be in their position have a few short cycles of rotation to make their fortune. It's no lie that being given such an opportunity would be a great temptation."

That would mean things on this damn planet were worse than just competition between other gangs...far worse. Sure, she'd voiced similar musings, but had held out on the belief she was wrong. How could they compete with such rampant corruption?

"If you're right, this is a big issue for our entire governmental system," she said.

"We're not trying to fix that today—we're trying to solve Macintosh's problem with letting a power-hungry sponsor take hold of their gang." Snapper's words were paired with enough venom to poison a grown human. If he'd been capable of it, she'd already be dead.

Bridget sighed. "I get that. So Macintosh breaks in at night, we storm this commissioner's office and break into a safe. Not hard."

"What's this Macintosh business? I said Full Throttle would help." Drag slapped a palm against the holo-table and the projection of the building frizzled for a moment.

"You and this group have already done enough. I mean, you've told me who to target and where. To ask for more is tempting fate. If we're caught, then the one punishable will be me."

Gina leaned in and bumped Bridget with her shoulder. The firm movement sent Bridget to the side a couple steps. "That's exactly why we need to help. Weren't you listening? They are trying to find a reason to remove you from power and place control of Macintosh in that sludge sack's hands. If you do get caught—which if we don't help, you will—then he gets what he wants and you lose. All of what we've sacrificed so far will be worth nothing."

"Sacrificed?" Bridget's outrage died as the last syllable left her mouth.

There were six pairs of eyes staring back at her and the faces that accompanied them carried various expressions of frustration.

"If you think we're not committed to this, you're wrong. The planning begins today, and we infiltrate tomorrow night. We regroup at dinner in the Watering Hole back room." Drag's words were the commands to spring everyone into action.

Gina and Snapper started to run possible infiltration routes, while Jack and Hemi discussed the best way to approach in the hauler. Rune was already outfitting bags for tools. Bridget watched in shock as everyone got down to business without questioning Drag or second-guessing his decision. No hesitation, no reluctance. These people he'd surrounded himself with trusted him completely.

She could dream of such devotion.

A hand clamped around her arm and she jumped as a small yelp escaped her lips.

"Come with me."

Bridget did her best to keep up with Drag's long strides, but still had trouble with her feet making the quick pace. She stumbled a couple times until Drag yanked her to him and lifted her up over his shoulder.

"What the hell are you doing?"

"Keeping you from injuring yourself," he replied, ducking down to ensure she didn't hit the door frame.

"I think that would be possible if you quit dragging me from rooms and trying to manhandle me instead of just letting me get from point A to point B on my own."

He stopped and tugged on her waist just enough to let gravity take over and her body slide off his shoulder and down toward the ground. She felt every muscle within his chest, his firm stomach and that hard as rock part of him she'd been begging for the night before.

Even in this tension-filled moment, he seemed to be aroused which was...*interesting*.

"Want me alone for other reasons?"

"Ignore that, and focus on this... Are you ready for what comes next?"

She frowned. "I would think it's obvious I am. I said Macintosh would handle the break-in and you ripped the opportunity from me."

But wasn't that how things always had gone between them, even in the past? Sure, she'd asked for help, but at the same time, she wasn't positive they could continue with this if she couldn't trust him not to abandon her again.

"Ah, so you are mad at me? What else?" Drag propped his hands on his hips and tapped a foot against the floor.

She was tempted to tell him those were her moves but thought better of it. "Of course, I'm mad. You said this wouldn't be awkward, that I would be safe. I'm feeling anything but..."

To say more would be admitting she'd spied and that made her legs a bit unsteady. Could she escape from Frog Lick if the situation required her to? Probably not with that monstrous tech room able to hack into almost everything.

"But? Be honest with me. That's how we start rebuilding this mess. Just tell me what I did."

She bit her lip, the internal debate forcing her to look for an exit strategy, but even as she turned in a circle, the reality of what she'd put herself in became enormous. *I'm at his mercy and I backed myself into a corner again.* There would be no going back, only pushing forward with the best intentions.

"I put a listener on you, and I heard what you said…what they said."

Drag stopped tapping, and she dared to glance up and make contact with that blue gaze of his. His expression had softened. There were no daggers being tossed her way nor a firm set to his lips.

"Bridget—"

"No, I don't want to hear the excuses, because that's all they will be. Don't try to console me with pretty lies when we both know the truth. You have to ally yourself to your people and me to mine. That's why I wanted to take over this next part. I don't want to risk whatever fragile peace between us by putting ourselves in a situation where one of us might have to choose."

Drag hooked two fingers under her chin so she couldn't pull away. "That's the bravest thing I've heard you say ever."

"I'd rather be running for the door right now." Her knees were practically clacking against each other, she was trembling so hard.

"That's the amazing part, how you're strong enough to be this vulnerable." He leaned in and pressed a soft, slow kiss to her lips.

She blinked, then closed her eyes and enjoyed the sensation of his mouth on hers. Here she'd been angry, mistrusting, and he could chase those thoughts away by touching her such an intimate way. Though of course he had to nip at her bottom lip right before he pulled away. Her heart raced, arousal igniting her body like the spark to the start of an engine.

As he released her, she sighed and kept her eyes shut. "Drag, make this mean something besides me surrendering even more of myself to you. I feel like whatever happens, I'm not going to win in the end."

"Depends on what you're hoping to get. I thought you just wanted to free yourself and Macintosh from Moag. Is there something else?"

He would demand for her to admit her hopes and dreams aloud. Make her confess those deepest desires that she'd allowed to awaken but dared not speak. He had to know what last night had done to her, what this little game they'd been dancing around from the moment he'd suggested they fake an engagement was doing to the walls she'd thought she erected so successfully.

Instead, he acted as if he was clueless, and that reaction was why she locked her legs and shoved away the yearning she carried for him, to be his, to be forever his good girl and a part of his future.

Forcing her eyes open, she straightened herself and looked him head on. "No, you're right. Which is why we need to stay in control of this attraction between us. There's no future beyond our limited time together. Understand?"

"As clear as recycle. No strings, no plans, no expectations beyond the bit of stress relief we can provide to each other for now."

Ooh, if that phrasing didn't make her want to throw fists, or even hurl items at him. She'd been right to hold back, right to confront him about what she had overheard. Even as her heart cracked a tiny bit all over again, along the same seam that had broken it the first time, she found peace knowing exactly how Drag saw her.

Whatever false hopes she'd been holding toward a reconciliation vanished. They were in an alliance to defeat a common enemy and using this as an opportunity to clear out the lingering attraction they held for each other. At least that's what she'd keep telling herself every time her stupid heart tried to interfere.

"Excuse me?" Rune, Drag's younger brother peeked around Drag and gave a little wave. "Afraid I've done all I can here while everyone else is getting into the meat of the details. How about we give Bridget a tour of some of our facilities and she can ask questions?"

"Why would she want that?" Drag asked, a deep frown on his face.

Bridget mirrored his expression. "I think it's a great idea."

Because the last thing she needed was to get caught up in another kiss or aroused by familiar closeness. No, her focus should be business.

"Fabulous. You'll follow me?" Rune stepped around Drag and started for the door.

Bridget smiled at the always cheerful younger Michaelson and took off after him. If anything, maybe this would get him to realize that two could play the game he wanted to wage.

* * * *

Two hour later, she was brimming with new knowledge about hydroponics and the tech needed to provide a three-filter approach.

"You build the filters?" she asked before sipping from a tall glass of the freshest recycle she'd ever tasted.

"We do, with sandstone ore that's left over from mining the marsanium." Rune kept explaining and she marveled. They were using the very ore that was often discarded for filtering water, not once or twice, but three times.

"That's safe?"

Rune nodded. "It is, and we're seeing better health overall from the consumption. Not to mention the airponics. We shared that technology with you, but your crops will yield twice as much if you use this filtering method."

"Then, by all means, provide me with the directions and I'll take it back."

Drag cleared his throat. "The problem is you won't have workers to support the plant."

"What are you talking about?"

He'd barely said two words since he'd followed her and Rune out of the mechanics bay. No, Drag had opted to watch and observe. This was the first comment he'd made.

"Women work the hydroponics bay. Well, women work everywhere, even in the mines if they so choose, but the bulk of our farming and hydroponics work is completed by women. If you don't involve the entire gang, this type of work can't be a success. The antiquated notions of male superiority aren't conducive to a gang's future."

Aren't I aware of that? Idiot.

She'd been the one to tell Drag the same thing all those years ago when they were dating, explaining her goals to drive Macintosh toward a new era once she'd taken over. But then...reality was difficult when faced with those who didn't trust her.

"Well aware. We've already started to integrate some women into positions that are more group related. We have groups that manage shoes, clothes and even minor house repairs. It's not quite the same, but I imagine if I can give them a taste of this"—she held up the glass in her hand—"they'd be open to an all-hands situation."

"The women handle house repairs?" Drag's tone implied he didn't believe her.

She thrust out her hands, palms up. "These calluses weren't developed from sitting in my house all day ruling. I help them as well. We've repaired heating elements, pipe assembly for waste output and even cooling boxes. I'm teaching them the things I taught myself because those men in the mines and the shipping buildings come home so damn exhausted there's no time or patience for such tasks. The women saw that need. The men were thankful their women were no longer complaining."

Rune looked up from one of the hydroponics filtration tubes. "Then they don't know?"

"Most likely they don't. If they do, they aren't saying anything. It's not immediate change, but it's a start."

She was prepared for them to laugh at her, cut her down. Because they'd demanded things be different here in Frog Lick and had succeeded. For her, it had been subterfuge and a slow attack at the misogynistic way of life from positions where it was already weak. Things were proceeding at a pace some would consider stifling, though every success was a win. Every time a woman came to the meeting stating how she'd been successful at learning something new without getting beaten for it was a victory.

"That's ingenious, Bridget," Rune said as he clapped her on the shoulder. "Can't wait to tell Petal. She'll be shocked to the core. Speaking of, I've got to meet up with her and help her haul a load to the Watering Hole for tonight. Sorry to run, but I'll be at the regroup."

Rune left the room then, the door to the bay closing with a heavy *creak* and slam in his haste to leave. Bridget, on the other hand, couldn't speak, as she looked over to the point where Rune had disappeared. She'd expected the worst and been greeted with the exact opposite.

"He's got an uncanny knack for saying the thing a person least expects. For being encouraging instead of insulting. It's been annoying me since we were kids and even more so when we arrived here. Thought we'd be stuck under the Smiths' thumbs for life, that I'd never get the opportunity I have today, but Rune... He never stopped believing." Drag's words were soft-spoken, but enough to get Bridget to turn and face him.

"He's braver than me, to live with such faith that the world will right itself. I'm not a revolutionary and my place as leader since my father's death has always been precarious, so my steps had to be little ripples in a pool of water, barely noticeable until it was too late."

Drag sighed. "Even when complimented, you down yourself and your efforts. I don't know the battles you've had to wage since I left, but from the conversations I've been a part of, I imagine they were numerous and exhausting. Everywhere you turned was the possibility of people working against you and still you found a way to enact some sort of change. Don't downplay those good works. Embrace them and own them."

He didn't say what he would have before. So she said it. "Because I'm Bridget fucking Macintosh."

"Yes." He grinned. "You are."

Chapter Twelve

Everyone was in the room, food consumed, drinks in hand. For the most part, all the awkwardness from earlier in the day had dissipated. Of course, Snapper sat at the far end of the table with Gina, and Bridget at the opposite end. But both Rune and Petal were engaging with her.

The others, Hemi, Shannon and Jack, sat talking intermittently, but overall Drag could appreciate this tentative peace, which had seemed impossible a few weeks prior. They didn't need to be best friends with Bridget to accomplish their goals. Alliances were made without the allies ever occupying the same room, so this was a big win in his opinion.

Though he found this moment nice, he was still struggling with the revelations of the day... How Bridget had listened in on his conversation with Jack and Snapper, the fact she had confessed what she did but then had labeled everything between them as a convenience. He could have thrown her across the room then, so frustrated at the fact she wouldn't open up. She was still running scared.

Was that why she had chosen against him when they were younger?

"All right, hope everyone got plenty to eat. It's time to regroup on the plan," Drag announced. The voices quieted, everyone looking at him. He was used to the staring, all eyes focused his way, but with Bridget here it was different.

She hadn't seen him lead before, until now.

"Jack, what's our route?"

"We leave an hour before sundown. We'll travel to the opposite edge of Wespero territory, to the area where all three meet, and we enter from the Wespero side, but we'll exit on the Aurora side of the building. Helps throw people off the scent in case anyone tries to determine which territory we came from. Drop-off occurs about an hour after sundown. Pickup is about thirty minutes after. We drive two haulers, with matching pattern formation so that no one can tell it's two."

Solid plan.

"Who's driving?"

"Myself and you. Snapper will take over while we're inside. We can't use Hemi. In case we're caught, we need Aurestral to have full plausible deniability."

Hemi chuckled. "And my wife would kill me if I didn't come home tomorrow morning. I'm already staying a day longer than planned."

"Why did you do that?" Bridget asked, because she couldn't leave well enough alone.

Hemi's grin became a little more wicked and Drag wanted to shout, but kept himself under control. He had to pretend to be unaffected and stop worrying about protecting Bridget all the time. She could handle the mess herself since she kept wanting to get these kinds of conversations started.

"Heard you were coming for a visit and I had to see this bullshit with my own eyes."

Bridget's color went a shade lighter. "I see. Hard to believe Drag would ally himself with the enemy."

"And not get revenge for himself and all the others who were damaged by you, yes."

Sweet heavens, give me a muzzle. This could erupt into a battle in a heartbeat, here in the very room where he wanted those leaders of Full Throttle and visitors to come together.

"And what's to say he still won't? I wouldn't judge him too harshly yet. There's a chance he could stab me in the back any second. I'm prepared if that's the case and… I'm sorry."

Hemi pushed back his chair, scraping the legs across the cement floor. "Excuse me?"

"The explosion wasn't supposed to happen. The engine was supposed to shut down. Something went wrong, a factor we hadn't taken into consideration with the NiteOx. Regardless, I never meant for you to—"

"Lose half my body? Be turned into a damn monster? Thank goodness I'm still loved, and able to find my own path in this messed-up future, but if you're looking for forgiveness you won't find it here." Hemi stood and started to march for the door. Drag attempted to stop him.

Hemi shrugged him off. "No, Drag, not this time. I already know what they plan to discuss. It's a solid setup. You don't need me here because I'll seem to keep things tense. I'll be out front with Gaia."

"I'll join him," Shannon said before pressing her lips to Jack's. Then she marched out as well.

Drag threw his hands in the air. "Hell, anyone else? Snapper? Gina? Jack? Why don't the rest of you quit and run as well? Bridget and I can figure this out ourselves. I get it, but I'm not asking you to forgive her."

"And I'm not asking either," Bridget said. "All I want is the chance to get rid of Cheatham. Thank you for helping me. I can't change the past, and I'm not asking you to forget it happened."

"Good, because those two won't ever," Jack said, pointing at the door both Hemi and Shannon had left through. "The kind of damage you inflicted leaves scars, some that may never heal. I only lost a pinky, but the rest of them…"

As he trailed off, Drag took in the heavy silence in the room. They'd started strong, then fallen apart. Maybe Bridget was right. A future between them would be too dangerous. All this bad blood hovering here… Words couldn't easily mend the poison her past actions had spread.

"Let's continue." Drag came closer to the table, twisting a chair around and sitting down so his arms rested over the back. "Tell us how we're breaking in."

Gina took a swallow of her drink before she started talking. "Easy enough, you'll wear a camera, and Bridget will continue to use her earpiece, which I'll hack into. Once you're inside —"

"You knew and said nothing." *Fuck.* Gina had known about the damn listening device.

"I believe a woman should know what the hell three men are saying about her behind her back." She patted

Snapper on the shoulder. "Sorry, but it's not nice for someone to walk into a dangerous situation unaware."

Snapper shrugged. "Not going to fight you there. Go on."

Drag was surprised at this momentary defiance on Gina's part. He believed the AI was backing them with her support, but like his brother Rune, Gina would sometimes make decisions that surprised him.

"You'll travel to the fourth floor, no lift because of cameras, which leaves the stairs. We'll have to time this precisely due to guard watch patterns, but it should be simple. The fourth door on the left from the stair entrance. I have a lock display EMP that will solve any issues, and no one will know that you've entered the room.

"Once inside, you'll access the safe in the floor, underneath the desk. I'll be able to feed Bridget details on how to get it open once I see it, so I'll need Drag there and Bridget close by. We open it, take all contents and you'll replace with several folders containing a few of my favorite old Earth nursery rhymes and a few limericks."

Bridget fidgeted in her seat.

"What's wrong with the plan?" Drag asked.

"Nothing, except what happens when the commissioner finds the documents missing? It doesn't help if we have them, and he doesn't. We have no proof that he committed the treason or was arranging to depose of anyone. Our accusations will turn into a case of jealousy and make me or even Drag look horrible. I'm not sure if this is the right approach."

Bridget's concerns were valid. How often did other gangs complain of corruption among the commissions then get dismissed because they didn't like how a race turned out or that another gang got a contract because of a better build? There were so many petty squabbles that it would be easy to see their argument as nothing but more of the same.

"That's where you're wrong," Gina replied. "We have to get the information to determine what they were doing from the get-go. We know there was conspiring. We know that funds had to change hands. A commissioner wouldn't act without lining his own pockets with crinkle. But the finer details will tell us how to take them down. Once we make copies of the documents, Snapper and I will return them on a separate visit."

Bridget stood up. "No, I can't ask that of you."

"We're not asking for permission," Snapper retorted. "We'll be the least susceptible and have a good reason for going there in the first place as we have to a submit a monthly mining and sludge refining report, same as the other gangs. It would be suspicious if you or Drag showed up for that. Not to mention a second break-in mere days before the race is too much of a risk."

Drag noticed how Bridget locked her fists at her sides. Funny how hard she was objecting against the man she tried to kill. "But still—"

"I've learned one thing over the last year of working alongside this man—once he's made up his mind, that's it." Gina's outburst got Bridget back in her seat.

Drag did his best not to chuckle. Gina was right. Snapper could be a stubborn jerk about things. The AI had been given a second chance when his superstitious friend didn't believe in them.

"Then we have a plan and we're prepared to execute it. Anything else?" Drag asked, eager to get this over with. He wanted Bridget alone…a growing desire to be close to her had built to ridiculous levels since he'd hauled her out of Gina's tech room. His focus was shot, knowing that in less than a week they would have to finish their alliance and that meant no longer being with her.

"No, I don't think so," Rune offered up first as he stood and extended a hand to his wife Petal. "We'll meet everyone at the mechanics bay tomorrow evening before send-off."

The pair exchanged farewells with Bridget and made their way out of the room. Snapper, Jack and Gina were talking amongst themselves.

"Do you need anything?" Drag asked.

Snapper waved him away. "Just go. You're useless to us right now. We'll see you both at the bay, by midday. I want you to see the maps, not just hear us talk about the ideas."

"Sounds good." Drag immediately stood, not caring that the chair he sat on clattered to the ground. Snapper knew where his mind had wandered. Its full focus was bent on getting Bridget back to his rooms and naked beneath him.

He hovered over her for a minute, and she sat there staring into her cup where the last remnants of recycle were sitting.

"What do you want from me now?" Her voice held a bit of annoyance and resignation, sure signs she despised how things weren't going the way she'd like them to. This new version of her, interested in self-sacrifice, amused him a tiny bit.

"I'd like you to consider giving up your body to me for the evening."

She glanced up, her gaze darting between those remaining in the room and him. "I don't think this is the appropriate time."

"You want more privacy?" he asked with a grin. His limbs itched, and he flexed his palms to chase away the incessant urge to just pick her up and toss her over his shoulder again.

"Didn't say that, just figured we should be more circumspect around others."

He crouched down in front of her to allow him to whisper. "I think they already know I've wanted to fuck you for the last twenty minutes. I'm done with conversation and looking for a good girl to take to bed. Are you that girl?"

She swallowed hard then nodded. "I am."

"Then follow me out of this room right now and keep up. I'm not stopping until there is a room with a bed in it."

Chapter Thirteen

Drag placed his hand over his mouth, trying to cover up the yawn working its way loose, but Gina caught it right away.

"Is this instruction boring you?"

"No… Sorry, Gina. Didn't sleep all that great last night."

Snapper chuckled. "Fucking tends to do that."

Gina slapped the table with a thin wooden reed, one she'd been using as a pointer, and everyone shut up, though Bridget's face was still covered in a nice blush. Drag shouldn't have liked that so much, but last night had been another adventure in exploring their re-ignited chemistry.

She'd been wild, eager and willing to follow every command. He loved her receptivity to letting go, doing as she was told. He caught her eye and mouthed the words 'good girl', enjoying how she flushed more.

The reed slapped the table again. "This is an important operation. Every moment spent in flirtation and arousal reduces our chance of success by ten percent."

"A bit high, Gina. I'd imagine actual fucking might increase by ten percent. Should we try?" Drag couldn't help but make the joke. He was in a damn good mood regardless of where they were headed or the danger involved. Somehow Bridget and their connection had always done that to him, made him feel damn near invincible.

"Are you taking this seriously?" Gina asked through clenched teeth.

"As serious as a racer behind the wheel in the championship. Show us the maps."

Gina sighed. "You're as bad as a particular runner I know, but let's continue."

Half a solar hour later, Jack and Snapper were loaded in one hauler with Drag and Bridget in the other, racing across the terrain, dodging vegetation and rock formations. The sun set behind them, casting various hues of orange and red across the sky.

Drag adjusted his grip on the steering wheel, the dust cover on his face only in place for Bridget's sake. He didn't want her to feel uncomfortable having to bundle up in goggles and the covering to protect herself from the sun and the dust. He didn't need that type of protection, but around certain people, he put up the façade to make them less intimidated by him. The nanites in his system had worked miracles, including giving him the ability to overcome weaknesses other humans couldn't.

Bonus, it gave him an excuse to stay quiet. While he was eager to talk to her, he was also a mess about what to say. They'd talked a little this morning, her sharing more stories of Macintosh's struggles and how their sponsorship had turned into a crutch that she had to depend on instead of an opportunity to grow and have her gang prosper. The conversations had made his blood boil for multiple reasons, but the question still remained… The one she hadn't bothered to answer yet. It was starting to eat at him. Why?

If Moag had been a horrible option, the wrong choice, why had Bridget turned to the sponsor, killed her father, attacked Snapper… *Makes no sense.* Drag had his guesses, but he was wanting to hear confirmation.

Because her in this seat beside him was right—his very marrow told him that much. He'd never felt more alive than with her next to him again. Sure, Snapper would say that was his dick talking, but he didn't believe it was mere sexual attraction. There had to be more here, right?

At the same time trusting her, this alliance, might break the fabric of his gang. Hemi, who was still an honorary member, couldn't let the past lie and neither could Shannon. The others were holding on out of blind loyalty but Drag could sense they would turn at the slightest provocation. The fact Bridget had received a communication right before they departed didn't help much either.

The Inccukai, she'd said, an inquiry about her whereabouts and when she would be back. Moag required her presence. *Fucking bastard.*

They'd barely left without an escort. How long before that assassin came poking around for her? Drag had already worked up a story for Snapper when they returned if the damn mummy came looking for them.

"Are you all right?" Bridget asked with her hand half resting on his cybernetic forearm. Her touch resonated throughout his body, the warmth, the connection.

"Yeah." Because be damned if they got into a deep conversation right now. Foolish of him for even considering it. They needed their focus on the mission, on the papers, the proof that Moag was manipulating half of Wespero by buying out the commissioner. "Just reviewing the plan, replaying the maps in my mind. Doesn't help us if we get lost. Gina already dialed into your ear piece?"

Another reason to be quiet. He didn't need his entire gang to know what he said to Bridget. Their conversation was for them alone. The others deserved answers too, but outside of Snapper, the others hadn't lost what he had...an entire planned future. He adjusted his grip again and let his foot ease off the accelerator.

"She said she'd only activate when we reached the commissioner's office. I believe her."

"You don't trust most people and you'll trust Gina after a couple interactions?"

Bridget removed her sun goggles as the night sky started to take over with its hues of purple. The sun was almost gone. "Yes. She didn't sell me out when she knew damn well I had planted a listening device. How she knew, I'd be interested in learning, but I can respect a woman is due a few secrets. She does what's right, without a second thought. I wish I was more like her."

They both grew silent again and Drag let things stay that way until they reached the commission office. As planned, Snapper took over for Drag. Both he and Jack drove off with haulers as if they were just passing through. Bridget and Drag moved up the stairs, communicating with simple hand signals.

Gina dialed in as Bridget cued up directions on when to use the EMP unlock device. The simple card-shaped item was covered on one end with rubber so it wouldn't short-circuit Drag's cybernetic components.

"Touch the other end and we're screwed. Make sure it goes back in the rubber case as well. Can't risk harm to any of us." She'd offered that good piece of advice before they'd left. Drag had suggested brute strength to get them inside but was reminded how this was a clandestine mission. They need to leave no speculation and no trace.

Once inside, it was lefts, then rights, up a couple flights of stairs, hiding in an alcove to evade passing guards and finally to the door of the Wespero commissioner, Paulos. Drag placed the card against the lock and two seconds later, the electric lights disappeared and the lock disengaged. *Just like the front door.*

"She's a genius," Bridget whispered as they slipped into the room and shut the door. Without the lock in place, they would have to manually block it.

Drag grabbed a small cabinet from against the wall and placed it front of the door.

"That's not the best idea."

He growled at Bridget. "We don't have anyone to stand guard. Now get your ass over here and let's look at this safe."

They moved the desk chair but couldn't move the desk with all the shit the commissioner had set on it, stacks of papers and junk. This idiot was a hoarder, if the cluttered way his room was arranged implied such a thing.

The floor-tile cover popped up with a simple compress motion, as Gina had predicted. When they lifted it up on its hinge, it revealed three dials and an electrical pad.

"Gina wants a closer look. Lean in."

Drag lowered his torso as close to the floor as he dared. He already felt claustrophobic and vulnerable in this position. What if Bridget tried to stab him? Old fears were starting to rise to the surface. He angled his head to see her, and she was all concerned at whatever instructions Gina was providing.

"What's wrong?"

"It's more complex than what she thought, but...not impossible."

Shit. "We're going to miss our escape window if this carries on. Can't we just use the EMP?" Drag reached for the case in his pocket.

"No!" Bridget's voice echoed through the room before she clapped her hands over her lips. "Shit... I'll be quieter, but Gina says you do that, and an alarm will trigger. Hands off the card. Give her a minute."

Drag gave himself a little more space, tapping his fingers against the floor.

"She said to stop that. Quiet waiting." Bridget braced herself with hands on her knees, crouched next to him. "You don't think he already knew somehow? That one of the others, maybe Hemi, said something?"

"Never, not even for all the crinkle in the world. Are you sure that listening device of yours hasn't already been hacked by the assassin working for Moag?"

She frowned. "No one knows I have this and don't try to accuse me."

"Well, you're blaming people I trust with my life, so it swings both ways here."

"Shh," she replied, placing a finger to his lips. He was damn tempted to bite it.

"Gina says it's intimidating, but quite simple in operation. Turn the top dial to the number one, the bottom to three and the middle to seven. In that exact order. Then press the symbol of a circle, diamond and square at the same time."

Drag followed the instructions as provided, though he said a silent prayer that this would work as he pressed the buttons. The safe's light turned from red to green and he dared to grab the handle. A quick ninety-degree turn, then the door opened. Within were the papers that Gina had spoken of, several folders and other items. He opted to grab all of them and hand them back to Bridget as she passed off replacement ones for the time being.

Just as he shut the safe door, he could hear voices from outside on the approach toward the commissioner's office.

Bridget started to speak but Drag clamped a hand over her mouth. "Shhhh, they're out there," he whispered. "Gina, what's the probability they will check the door?"

He huddled Bridget close to him, the bulk of the bag strapped to her front holding the paperwork crushed between them, the easiest way to hear Gina's reply.

"Forty-five percent chance of door checks but increases to ninety-five if they notice the missing lock light. Also, you have five solar minutes left before your ride departs."

They were counting on the guards being too absorbed with their own conversation to pay close attention to what was happening. Bridget's heart rate picked up along with his. He could hear his pulse in his ears. They stood stock still embracing each other. Though his cock was already starting to wake up and ask what was happening, Drag's eyes were glued to the door handle, waiting for the end to drop.

When the handle moved up and down, that signaled the end.

"I love you," he whispered.

They were going to be caught, arrested, and Cheatham would have what he needed to remove Bridget from leadership of Macintosh. She'd erred in trusting Drag and Full Throttle. Made the mistake of believing she could take on this kind of scheme herself and they weren't that good.

Nor were they assassins or spies trained to do this type of work. The door handle jiggled, and she held her breath, squeezing Drag tighter with her arms.

"I love you." The whispered words in her ear threw her into shock and her chest grew tight. She tried to push Drag away, but he wouldn't let her go.

Then a guard spoke about the door lock being busted, but the door didn't budge. Things were fine — they'd alert maintenance in the morning. The pair of footsteps moved away and only after she could no longer hear them did Drag release her.

"Three minutes until they leave. The guards are all in positions away from the stairwell. You have a clear path."

Bridget was still reeling from Drag's declaration. How could he unleash such words on her at a time like this? The worst possible time, when they were about to be caught and now... The damn idiot had moved the cabinet back to its position, but he'd left the tile open on the floor.

Leaning down, Bridget replaced everything to ensure the floor was as it had been when they arrived.

She slid the desk chair back in place then her body was on autopilot, knowing their window for escape was closing.

Drag opened the door and turned, motioning to her. "Let's go."

She picked up her pace and ran, past him and out through the door into the hall. The stairway wasn't far—one quick right turn, and they'd make the stairwell. She did her best to keep herself on the tips of her toes, light and fast steps as she made her way down one, two and three flights of stairs. With no idea if Drag was behind her, she ran as if his words were chasing her out of the building.

He loved her…even after everything she'd done? He was speaking madness, driven by the desperation of the moment. Even so, the emotion lodged inside her heart, the beats echoing within her, as she grasped onto that confession, wanting to hold it tight. She'd give almost anything for the statement to be true, but the time to ask wasn't now as they fled the commission building.

The door that entered into the main foyer was in front of her. She could hear Drag's steps behind her on the steps.

"Stop," Gina's voice echoed in her ear. "Wait ten seconds, then go."

She was tempted to ask why but didn't dare. The woman speaking through her ear piece was an enigma who had some sort of magical talent with technology and knew things most humans would not even dream. So, Bridget halted and held up her hand to get Drag to slow his pace. Her heart raced and she was damn sure if anyone walked by the stairwell they'd hear it. He came up short beside her as she finished her countdown.

"Go." Gina yelled in her ear right as she reached one.

Bridget pushed open the door, with Drag crowding in behind her. The damn fool lifted her up, then hoisted her over him, crushing her body against his. How the hell he kept his footsteps near silent even with the extra weight on his shoulder she wasn't sure. But they were out through the door in seconds and down the steps. He tossed her into the seat of the hauler, before ripping the shoulder bag off her and tossing it to Snapper.

The other racer disappeared into the night, and Drag was left driving them out of there, following. They were away from the commission office when she dared to speak.

"I can't believe you said that."

"What? Let's go? I mean, I couldn't whistle for your attention."

Bridget reached up and pulled the earpiece out of her ear, threw it on the floorboard and crushed it underneath her boot heel. Because be damned if anyone else was going to hear this conversation. She could imagine the anarchy his words might drum up if Gina shared them, but the rest of this needed to be kept between them alone.

"That's not what I'm talking about. You said, 'I love you'."

Drag jerked the wheel the tiniest bit, then course-corrected. "You must have misheard me."

"No, you were right next to me, and it was in my ear. I don't think I could mistake those words. Not when I've heard them from you before, a long time ago. Why?"

"I—"

"If you deny this one more time, I'm jumping out of this hauler, my safety be damned. I can't, Dakota." His real name had slipped out, but her entire body was like a compressed coil ready to launch over across the seat and kiss him. If those words... No, she couldn't believe in such fairy tales.

"There is never a right time to say them. But that moment, if I didn't get a chance, I wanted to say those to you again."

"Do you mean them?"

Dakota glanced in her direction, then slammed on the brakes. Her safety belt kept her from slamming into the dash though her palms slapped against the hard surface to provide extra bracing.

"Always." The single word tore away her misgivings and cynicism and brought tears to her eyes. She'd never believed anyone would love her again after what she'd done. Hell, he didn't even know the truth of everything and had still said them.

Undoing her safety belt, she crawled across the seat into his, then straddled his lap. The kiss she unleashed wasn't tentative or nice. It was all her passion and desire for him that had been curtailed over the years, everything she hadn't already shown him. He met her stroke for stroke, bite for bite. Arousal coiled deep inside her, rising until she was grinding on his rock-hard cock right there in the driver's seat.

Her head fell back as he nipped and sucked at her throat. Then he growled. "No fucking way am I not getting all of you and settling for your orgasm not being on my tongue."

As he hugged her close, she couldn't help but giggle as Drag clenched her against him with one hand while he drove the hauler off the main path with the other behind a couple large rock formations. It would give them a bit of privacy, but if a caravan...

"How do you want this?" He turned the hauler off, then leaned her back.

"I want to be spread out to you like a banquet."

He grinned at her and unclicked the latch that would release his safety belt. "Then get out and give me five minutes max. I'll handle this."

She left the hauler on the driver's side and Drag followed after her. Except instead of stopping to wrap her up in his arms and continue what they had started, he moved to the back of the hauler. He popped open the tailgate, moved the rear seats down, then laid out three blankets. Only then did he come back to her side.

"I don't have pillows, but I think I can keep you comfortable."

"As long as I'm with you, I'll be happy." She said the words and meant them as she looped her arms around Drag's neck and let him lift her off the ground and carry her toward the rear of the hauler.

He set her down on the edge of the tailgate and removed her boots, then her pants and underwear. She was naked from the waist down and so very fucking wet. "Lean back and spread those legs for me."

She did as he asked and was rewarded with the slow slide of a thumb over her clit and down to her pussy entrance, along with a low whistle and Drag's soft-spoken, "Good girl."

There was no additional preamble, just Drag lowering his head between her legs as he hoisted said limbs over his shoulders and began to feast on her. She was nearly hanging upside down, the far top of her torso touching the back of hauler bed as he worked his tongue at first against her clit, then in and out of her pussy like an engine piston.

She tried to control herself but couldn't help but squeeze her muscles against his invasion. He growled in pleasure. In response, he bit at her inner thighs before continuing his assault on her clit. There was no way to describe this sudden, rapid rise of her desire. She was a panting, sobbing mess as he brought her to one orgasm, then another. His mouth had to be tired. Then again, his cybernetic components probably— *mother of Mars.*

She bit down on her lip to keep from screaming. When that wasn't enough, she bit her hand, but every nerve in her body was lit up like the racing dome in the middle of a championship. She was sure every animal or human within hearing distance knew how many times she'd come.

When the next one hit, she couldn't help but scream, then he was there, swallowing her cry with his mouth and tongue that tasted of her. In the middle of that frantic kiss designed to stifle her shout, his cock was already poised at her entrance. He took hold of her shoulders and used that grip to impale her on his cock.

She gasped against his mouth, then allowed their tongues to dance once more after the ease of his intrusion. He was everything firm, hot and delicious, sinking into her with such force she wanted it as hard as he could give her.

If he could somehow mark her this way, so everyone that looked upon her after this night would know that she belonged to him... No matter how stupid and foolish, she'd still wish for such a thing. Breaking the kiss, she turned her head to roughly whisper in his ear, "Fuck me like you'll never do so again."

She leaned back and looked up at the stars as he began to move, grinding into her as he did, letting her feel every part of his width and length. Then he moved his thumb to her clit and started to pick up the pace. His human hand pressed down on her collarbone and she was forced to look at him, to see the hunger for her reflected in his eyes, his pupils so wide and open. She gasped with each push and pull.

He was so gorgeous, the sweat dripping from his brow, the way he held onto her, and in return, she found the same words he'd given her bubbling up on her lips. But before she could utter them, he kissed her, smothering all sound as he came, and her final orgasm was wrenched from her body.

When he finally pulled away, pressing smaller kisses to her forehead and cheeks, the moment was so tender she feared she'd cry. He helped put her pants back on and her boots, then climbed into the hauler and lay down beside her.

It took but a single pat to his chest to get her to crawl into his lap and find solace and warmth among the chilly night in his arms. That was when she dared to return the words.

"I love you," she whispered, then let herself drift to sleep.

Chapter Fourteen

Bridget rode in the backseat of the Macintosh hauler beside Trio, her sun goggles firmly in place, already missing Drag more than she could dare speak. She couldn't discuss what had happened between them at all, which hurt.

They had slept out among the stars until the early morning, then come back into Frog Lick to be met by Trio guarding the entrance to the Full Throttle mechanics bay. The assassin had been denied entrance, but had refused to leave until Bridget had returned.

There was no discussion of where she'd been, though anyone with eyes could have guessed. *Thank goodness Drag had the forethought to give my bag to Snapper.* Trio had demanded they return to Macintosh straight away, orders from Cheatham, who was displeased with her being gone for more than a day with so many preparations needed ahead of the race.

A race we're not even going to be in.

Unless Cheatham had other plans to disqualify some of the main teams.

"Does he think Macintosh will race?"

The Inccukai might not answer, but at this point, they were her one window into Cheatham's plan, until Gina deciphered the documents she and Drag had stolen.

The cloth-covered human turned those red iris eyes on her, which in the daylight was almost as scary as how they glowed in the nighttime. "He wouldn't have come all this way if he didn't expect it to happen."

"If there's another explosion at a racetrack, even the day before, that could raise suspicions."

"Though everyone is playing with NiteOx because of Full Throttle, right? Who's to say if a gang was careless or not? We don't believe there will be an issue."

Another accident—how many lives was Cheatham willing to sacrifice now? "I don't want to be a part of this anymore. If we have to cheat, then we're not winning with our own talent and skill."

"That wasn't what you told us before. You said by whatever means necessary, a win is a win. Maybe Full Throttle is making you soft?"

"No, I'm tired of lives lost for no reason. They aren't hurting us. Not racing this year isn't hurting us. Our ship profits are higher than ever. The technology Full Throttle has supplied will make us able to turn even bigger profits by having healthy miners and engineers."

Trio shrugged. "We know nothing about what makes those things a success. We follow orders when they are given. Right now, you're to return and explain why you've been gone so long. If he requests it, we damage you. It's a simple transaction. You should have learned by now that this agreement means you bow to him, no one else. Our job is to ensure it."

Bridget chose silence for the remainder of the ride. Loyalty from the Inccukai depended on who could pay the mummy's fee and that wasn't her. She was stuck until she could escape again and go back to Frog Lick. She'd meet with Cheatham, then return. Her sponsor could get used to the fact she had unfinished business there.

* * * *

A couple of hours later, she was showered, dressed and walking into the guest quarters supplied to Cheatham. It wasn't just a single room. No, he had taken over an entire house that had housed two families… Families that had been loyal to her father.

That was yet another reason she yanked at the hem of her shirt and pursed her lips as she entered. "You called for me?"

No reason for her to begin posturing now. *Bridget fucking Macintosh bows to no one.* Drag hadn't forgotten he was the one who'd encouraged her empowerment. Gods, she missed him already. What she'd give to have him behind her, but it was best if he steered clear. They'd both agreed on that. He had to begin preparations for the race.

Cheatham turned to face her, wiping away the stain of grapes on his lips with a napkin. "Yes, you have returned. After I had to send an escort to be sure those Full Throttle heathens would give you back. For a moment, all of Macintosh started to believe you'd been kidnapped. I'm glad to see they were wrong."

Bridget crossed her arms. "Dead wrong. As I said before, I was touring facilities, gathering information and continuing this sharing of knowledge that Drag has promised with this alliance. He knows when he's beat. He needs this partnership to ensure they don't falter. His confidence that they will win the race is all bravado. You know how he is." Bridget dared to enter farther into the room, letting the door cover sweep back into place. The area was brightened by several windows, the coverings sheer to limit the sun's impact but still let light into the area. While it was warmer than her own quarters, she didn't want to be that closed off with him.

"Yes, though he's under this misapprehension you'll be his wife, when you know damn well our agreement is that you'll be mine. The time is up. I've come to claim my winnings from our pact twelve years ago. I let you play and try at being the ruler of this gang, but so many come to me daily with their frustrations."

Her blood was starting to boil. No way in hell would she be his wife. Killing her father was supposed to cancel that out, but instead he acted as if her murderous actions had served to postpone the inevitable. "We agreed if I removed my father, gave you more favorable terms, I was leader with no time limits."

"Ah, but there were other parts of that bargain, including killing your half-brother who still lives. Of course, you couldn't do it with an audience, and I was obliged to step in to defend you. You're in my debt. Marriage is how you'll repay me."

"No." Because debt or not, they'd had an agreement. He was their sponsor, not their ruler. With Drag's help, Macintosh could survive without him. "I refuse. You can pull your sponsorship. We're prepared to move on without you."

Cheatham grinned, the devilish look on his face chilling her. He'd looked this same way when she'd propositioned him twelve years ago. "But are they? I told you I've heard complaints. This isn't a lie. Imagine the outrage you'll receive when the shipping contracts are gone, when the food shipments stop coming in. They won't want you anymore. You'll be deposed."

"I'm not afraid to be without power anymore. Maybe they will pick a better leader, but at least they won't be under your thumb."

The space hole stalked across the room, his floor-length robes dragging across the floor, until he was standing inches from her. He could easily reach out and hit her, but Bridget stood her ground. If she'd just had the nuggets to kill him all those years ago, maybe her father would have listened to her then.

"You think that's how easy this will be? You walk away with no consequences? I'll blow that damn racer of Full Throttle's up right on the track. I'll ensure Macintosh is unaffiliated along with Full Throttle."

"No. No. No." Bridget repeated the word as she shook her head, because what he spoke of had to be impossible.

"Denying it doesn't mean I can't make it happen. I've made friends here, Bridget, on Mars, in almost every gang. They like it when I give them gifts, like the favors I can bestow. Though I don't sell my body like a whore. No, I'll leave those efforts to you."

She screamed, loud and unrestrained, the tears hot on her cheeks. Damn him, but it was her fault she'd allowed this monster a foothold here and he'd taken full advantage. She could care less about being called names, not when the evidence of her true curse was far more horrifying.

"Yes, I know about you and that Michelson. Fuck him as you like, but in a few days you're mine and only mine. If you don't submit, then watch me take everything away."

Bridget swiped at her face. "Why the hell are you doing this?"

"Because I can. I won't lie—seeing you forced to give in to me is going to make it all the sweeter." He pressed three fingers to his lips and kissed them.

She spit in his face then, unable to contain her rage but at the same time limited in how she could react. A part of her still wanted to live. She'd been prepared to give it all up walking into that house, ready to cast aside the future as Macintosh leader for a chance of a smidge of the happiness she'd experienced being with Drag again.

But she should've known better—there were no happy endings for people who made deals with devils. Cheatham was a spawn of some demon and she needed to ensure his destruction. Killing him would result in her death or a life shoved away in a prison sell... *Or worse, as a fuel sacrifice.*

She settled for spittle then turned and ran, out of the house, into the main square of Macintosh where she slowed her steps and tried to do the same for her breathing. The heavy pants from her rushing to escape weren't easy to quell and she found herself searching those who passed by for a friendly face.

She found none. No one here knew what she had gone through. Her sacrifices and struggles were unimportant to them. The gang members reacted when bothered or events affected them. Her grievances would fall on deaf ears here. She was backed into a cage once again, but this time one of her own making. She couldn't blame her father or anyone else. She'd made these choices.

Only last time you left him out of them.

There was one person she hadn't turned to before, and maybe this time she could trust him to help her out. Bridget moved to a hauler, telling those who balked at her driving alone that she didn't need anyone's help. She could do this herself and she'd return soon enough.

Driving out of town, she hoped she was making the right choice this time. Because she was out of friends, time and luck.

Chapter Fifteen

Drag had just left the mechanics' bay. The sun was long past set. He'd enjoyed a bowl of lukewarm stew brought over from the Watering Hole as he'd studied the race map that Gina predicted. The track changed with every race and every championship, but Gina and her damn AI brain had researched and logged every track type since the races had started. She developed a map based on the predictions of all the previous ones used.

Which she'd put in Drag's hands and told him to study, along with writing down his own plan for how to combat the obstacles. From there they'd tweak the racer to meet his needs, but damn if it hadn't been a full twelve plus solar hour day. He'd gotten straight to work after Bridget had been commanded back to Macintosh.

It had taken everything in him to hold back from launching into a fight with the damn assassin that had come to bring her home. He'd also been upset when she hadn't bothered to try to stay. She could have told the assassin to fuck off and the rest of them would've backed her.

Well, maybe not… but I would've.

He glanced at the stars above. The dome towering high off in the distance was dark. They'd be holding the championship there for the first time in three years. He'd won her before twelve years prior. A few days from now and he'd be putting himself on the line again, but this time the stakes were even higher. This was for Full Throttle and gaining a sponsor.

Not someone like Moag. No, there were others, ones who wanted to work with gangs and foster success… This he had to believe. He held out hope that all this hard work over the last couple years would pay off. Meanwhile, he also waited for Gina to tell them what she had learned from the paperwork. But the woman refused until Drag turned in his plan.

Of course, she and Snapper were holed up in her room when Drag had finished. No way was he knocking on that door and getting an eyeful. No, he wanted a certain fiery redhead, who he had no idea when he'd see again.

A star shot across the night sky and he wished on it like a fool.

Bring her back to me…soon.

He had managed to make his way to his house, a couple buildings down from Jack and Shannon's, when he heard the hauler speeding its way into town. The damn headlights flooded the streets and Drag immediately took a fighting stance, cybernetic fist set. If this was the Inccukai come back to finish him, damn it if he wasn't ready.

Instead, the hauler started to slow then came to a stop. The brightness from the headlights faded as they switched off, and there in the front seat was a windswept Bridget. She leaped out and ran toward him, jumping on him. He had no choice but to change his approach to cup her ass so she didn't fall.

She pressed kisses to his face all over, and saved his lips for last. "I'm so glad to see you. It was stupid how much of the day I spent trying to get here."

"I'm happy you're here too, though I didn't expect my wish to be answered so soon."

She angled her head and grinned. "What are you talking about?"

"Nothing. Ignore me. Let's get inside."

"What about the hauler?"

Drag shrugged. "Someone will take care of it."

He walked with her in his arms, loving the feel of her even if she was covered in a day of travel on the road. He was a sweaty mess from being in an office staring at possibilities all day. After her got her inside his place, he dared to ask for what he wanted right now.

"Maybe we shower first?"

She shook her head and pushed on his upper chest. "First, we need to talk. Can you put me down?"

Okay, maybe he should've been clear when he'd made his wish. He wanted her here and naked under running water. "Can it wait?"

"No, I need to talk about this without getting distracted by your body."

He let Bridget go, letting her slide down the front of him and get a good feel for the hard-on she'd be passing up. The grin on his face was uncontrollable as she rolled her eyes.

"That's what I'm talking about," she said as she grabbed his forearms and tugged him toward the pair of chairs he had in the main room of the house. "Sit with me for a minute and let me get this out there."

Drag went with her reluctantly, though concern started to overtake his arousal. "What's this about?"

"You wanted to know what happened back then, and I think I'm ready to tell you." She released him and took a seat, rubbing her palms against the top of her pant-covered thighs.

Did he let her keep going? He'd wanted to know the truth of that day for so long and part of him was desperate for details and at the same time could he handle whatever she said? The replay of Snapper and Jack asking him if he was prepared for this not to go his way made his chest grow tight.

He sat down in the chair beside her and place his hands flat on the armrests. "What prompted this?"

Because be damned if she didn't come to this decision by herself, no way. She'd been locked down for so long, even when he'd asked, and her change of heart sparked a snap of fear.

"Cheatham was waiting for me. He's threatening me all over again. I know I've created a monster that I'm not sure whatever we plan will get rid of, but you have to believe that I always meant for the best. Things weren't supposed to be like this."

"How?" Because what would more words do but prolong her storytelling? He could handle this. He'd lost an arm, undergone excruciating painful surgery for a cybernetic replacement, years of loneliness and frustration... *I can listen to what happened.*

"The day of the race, after you won, my father announced I would be marrying Cheatham. We'd gain him as a sponsor, but part of the agreement was my hand. It went against what you and I had planned, and I told my father so. I'd already decided, and he said that this would give me a better life, one I deserved."

This was the reason she hadn't come to see him straightaway after the race was over.

"I couldn't accept it. So, I decided to negotiate with Cheatham myself. If my father wouldn't hand over leadership to me, would Cheatham honor the agreement with a few adjustments? I wouldn't marry him The price was steep—he wanted a higher cut of the shipping profits, but would supply food and medicine as agreed. Then he demanded I pay with my father's life, because no way did he see Travis Macintosh stepping down. When I agreed, he told me it had to be by my hand, not a duel with a representative. I was stupid to say yes. I was so blinded by the thought I'd lose what we were working for, our future together, I was willing to pay any price."

Fuck. She was blasting him away because he knew how people like Moag operated. They didn't stop at one—they kept pushing for more and more every time they got anywhere.

"Also I had to agree to remove any potential claims to my position as leader, which meant Snapper. He was my father's bastard, but there were still those in Macintosh who would accept him in a heartbeat. Cheatham wanted no opposition if he was to give me this opportunity."

"What about your father?" Because she'd loved him. Sure, the man had been flawed and made a dozen mistakes, but—

"He refused to relent. I gave him a chance to change his mind. Told him how I loved you, how we had plans to make Macintosh into a thriving gang. No more fighting for scraps when it came to food or shipping contracts. But he said he'd already decided to turn the gang over to Snapper and he had given his word to Cheatham…and so had I."

Tears started to stream down her face, but her voice was calm and collected, as if she weren't confessing to the sins he'd been blamed for all those years ago. The worst part ripping at the very fabric of him — her goal in her actions had involved being with him.

"Then I came in and the plan fell to shit," he murmured.

"No, it was already going to shit," she said. "I told Cheatham I'd make it right, and you'd fall in line, but I couldn't find you. I figured you'd gone to Snapper's and then he was there sleeping, and I had a chance. Before you barged in…Cheatham took over then. I was devastated. You always said you'd have my side, that you'd believe in me but you…" Her voice cracked, rivers of water running down her cheeks and neck, soaking her shirt. She was a mess, but then again there was dampness on his own cheeks.

Heavens, this hurts so fucking much. He clenched his fists and rubbed away the evidence of his own emotions.

"I turned against you. I had to speak out. Bridget, you should have talked to me sooner. If I'd known before you took action…" Except those words were pointless because Moag would have made sure she was alone. People bent on power ensured their marks were desperate and willing to act without assistance. That was how they won.

His stomach clenched again. There were still a few unanswered questions. "Was it your idea to blame me?"

She shook her head. "No, as I said, Cheatham made the decisions then. I was at his mercy because he was saving me from a certain death. I'd messed up and now for his kindness I would be even more entrenched. That's how I ended up dug in so deep and with that horrifying Inccukai at my side."

The door burst open at that moment, and the very thing she'd been speaking of seemed to manifest from the darkness. "When you call us, we're willing to come. Bridget, our master would like you to return as soon as possible."

Every bit of anguish and pain swirling through his body pooled together in his gut. A righteous ball of anger propelled him out of his seat, his steps heavy and cracking the wood floorboards beneath them. He usually controlled his strength, but in this moment, he let the full force of what he was capable of tear loose.

Drag had just passed Bridget's chair and she was already latching onto his human forearm with both hands.

"Please, let's run. Don't fight. I can't lose you."

He grinned at her. "You're not going to. Stay back."

He shook her loose with a gentle jiggle while forcing the chair across the room, and farther out of reach of this bandaged-up assassin.

"This is pointless. We are capable of far more feats than simple acts of strength. If you fight us, you will die."

"Then good thing I'm not afraid of death," Drag said as he balled up both fists and threw his cybernetic one first, straight at the Inccukai's head. Of course, the bastard dodged. A flurry of fabric was the only thing remaining as they moved.

Drag could feel the hits they landed. His one misthrown punch opened him up to attacks, open palm and finger jabs to different parts of his anatomy. If he'd been a regular human, he'd have fallen to his knees, but his cybernetics absorbed the shocks and dispelled them.

He laughed. "That's it. So much for impressive skills. My body doesn't work like those you're used to assassinating. Now hold still."

A quick duck and sweep of his leg knocked the Inccukai to their back. Drag launched upward, to bring a knee down right on their solar plexus, but the assassin rolled out of the way. They continued to move, circling the room as they did so, trading jabs, kicks and an occasional punch. Drag landed a couple, but anyone watching would have thought he was losing.

The Inccukai had pulled out a pair of small blades that they kept between the knuckles of their hands. The tiny cuts were piling up and Drag was bleeding from twenty different spots. He didn't feel fatigued, but more frustrated than anything.

"It's kind of stupid to fight someone who has the stamina to outlast you."

The Inccukai lashed out again, this time slashing at Drag's cheek, and landing the delivery. "Funny you mention such an important part of a battle. Did you know there is a plant on Mars, a rawei cacti. It's a cactus that survives because it poisons any creature that comes in contact with it. Our order is one of the few that bother to harvest the rawei cacti and we coat our blades in its poisonous power."

Rawei... Rune had mentioned the plant before. The poison could also be used as a deterrent to keep wildlife from their plants. Wild animals despised the scent of the rawei. *Maybe because it kills them.*

Such types of attacks didn't work on him, since the nanites in his system tended to metabolize anything that entered his bloodstream at a faster pace than a regular human... except he'd started to feel a bit sluggish. His motions were a tiny bit slower than before.

"How fast does it kill?"

"All dependent on the levels of poison in your system."

"No!" Bridget cried out. "Please stop. I'll go with you."

"You're not going anywhere, Bridget. Stay back and I'll take care of this shitty excuse for a killer." Drag growled his frustration and charged again.

This time he managed to get a hold of a fistful of the damn bandages covering the assassin from head to toe. He tugged and the bindings snapped, falling away. The sight was hideous, burned white and pink skin underneath, scarred flesh still in stages of healing.

The Inccukai groaned. Drag wasn't sure if the exposure had weakened them somehow, but he was willing to keep whittling away at the cloth coverings if that meant he'd have a chance to slow this bastard down. This time, Drag opted for the head covering. He pulled it away, but the wrapped head was still an obstacle.

Before he could pivot and begin another attack, the Inccukai plunged one of the small blades into his collarbone. "Die, half-human scum."

"Funny, you're about as human as I am," Drag replied as he dropped to one knee and coughed violently. Blood pooled in his mouth. The wound wasn't good. He reached up and ripped the knife out. "One difference is I didn't sell my soul to get abilities. I let them give me an arm for the one I lost."

The Inccukai planted a foot in Drag's face. "That last one is fatal with the poison so close to your heart. A soul is worth nothing to a dead person."

Drag glanced up, hoping that Bridget wasn't trying anything stupid. Yet there she was, her arms bound by the Inccukai's one hand, while the assassin's other hand yanked at her red hair hard enough to make her cry out.

I have to get to her.

She'd confessed the truth, even if it was horrifying to know how deep she'd fallen in the muck and mess. How she hadn't trusted enough to come to him before making such rash decisions. No way would he allow this assassin to steal his chance to… *Damn it, I still love her even with all crazy.*

He shoved himself up on his knees. His vision was already starting to go a bit wonky, shirt now stained in blood. There were merits to removing that knife and some problems, too. "Let. Her. Go."

"Why won't you die already?" the Inccukai asked as they lifted up Bridget by her hair.

She screamed. "Help! Help us. Someone." Her words were punctuated by sobs and painful cries. Her hair had to be tearing from her scalp. She tried to fight back with her arms and legs, but no luck. The damn assassin exhibited a ridiculous amount of strength.

If this was the end for him and Bridget, no way wouldn't he say what he needed to. "I love you, Bridget fucking Macintosh. Don't ever forget it. No matter what stupid idea you get in your head. I love you."

That was when a sharp whistle rent the air, followed by three more—all of them knives flying through the room then piercing the Inccukai. The assassin roared, dropping Bridget to the floor, then charged toward Drag. Except not toward him, at someone else behind him, in the doorway that he couldn't see.

He forced himself to pivot on his knees—perfect timing, as the assassin was at knee level as well. Their surprise savior had already plucked out one of those glowing red eyeballs with a blade.

"I told you, Wren. One day, I'd find you and I'd kill you. Funny how this whole time you weren't so very far away."

"Lee." The name came out on a guttural sputter from the Inccukai.

Then the woman in question, her long black ponytail whipping back and forth, climbed atop the Inccukai's shoulders, flexing her thighs around assassin's neck.

"Last words...I don't care to hear them." Lee snapped the assassin's neck then hopped off.

Drag couldn't feel more than relief. With the reprieve, he fell forward and passed out.

Chapter Sixteen

Bridget had been unable to take her eyes off Drag since the attack. She'd been foolish charging off here and not expecting Cheatham to put a tail on her. Of course, the bastard wanted to ensure she wasn't running away.

Drag had almost been killed. But not…no, the woman who'd shown up and saved them, Lee, had produced an antidote to the rawei cacti. Drag had been patched up and Gina reassured Bridget that his wounds would heal in mere hours.

"Nothing a few nanites can't fix."

"What about more killers?" She'd been a tear-stained, headachy, panicked mess. Her adrenaline was the one thing keeping her going.

"We've got guards posted everywhere now. Lee will stay on patrol around the house. You couldn't be safer." Gina had departed then, and Bridget had stayed, keeping vigil over Drag. As the hours passed, she dared to examine the room.

Drag appeared to live a spartan existence. There wasn't much by way of decorations on the walls. The bed was simple with a sheet, blanket and two pillows, nothing like her overstuffed mattress. His clothes all hung neatly in a closet, and there were no chairs, just a small bedside table with a lamp.

She'd dragged in a chair from his kitchen just to stay close to him. Then she'd noticed the box underneath his bed. Unable to stop herself, once she had confirmed he was still asleep, she leaned down and pulled the box out, extra-careful as she opened the flaps, though she barely contained her gasp.

Inside were the memories they'd shared, notes she'd written sealed with the press of her color-stained lips. A near empty bottle of her perfume, which she'd given to him full, telling him to spread it on his sheets and pillow whenever he missed her. There were a few photos taken at various races, all with her hanging on his arm. There were also the drawings. Once upon a time, she'd spent hours each day drawing everyone and everything she could, from racers to ships to people. There were a couple books of hers she'd left with Drag because drawing wasn't considered a skill she needed.

Here they were, parts of her past all shoved into a container and hidden away for years. *Shit*. She flipped through the pages, lost in the memories of her life long gone.

"Snapper said I should have burned it all, cleared away anything we shared, but I couldn't bring myself to do it. And I'm glad I didn't... You look like you used to, staring at those pictures."

Her gaze snapped to his as she dropped the book back in the box and scrambled off her chair onto the bed. "Are you okay? How are you feeling? Are you thirsty? I can go get water, food, a cold rag. Tell me."

She was reaching to touch him, pressing her hand against his forehead, and another to his chest to feel his heartbeat. He'd been asleep for most of the night. It was still the early hours of the morning. "You should be resting."

"Wow, I should have fought someone and got stabbed sooner. I like it when you fawn all over me." Drag chuckled as she continued her inspection.

"That's not funny. I was scared shitless. I thought you were going to die." She'd been two words from collapse if anyone had told her Drag wasn't going to recover. Snapper had even backed away when he had seen her acting feral and ridiculous. "I refused to let anyone near you except Gina and Lee. Those women are my saviors. I owe them my life."

"I think that's the opposite way around." He was still smiling. For a heartbeat, she took that in, the fact he was grinning and happy even after he'd almost bled out and died from poisoning.

That was when she was one-hundred percent sure that she loved him, maybe more than she had before. The love was the same, yet new, like a rebuilt racer after a crash. There were a lot of the same parts, but also new ones to solidify things and make them better, stronger. Before she could think twice, she muttered, "I love you." Then she mashed her lips to his.

His desperation seemed to match her own. Their lips and tongues melded together as if they couldn't get enough of each other. They tried to devour one another, almost like the last couple weeks hadn't happened. But her desire for closeness and connection was all driven from the fear she could have lost him, and joined by her love for him defending her.

His hands were already moving, tearing apart the shirt she wore, exposing her breasts to the cool air. "You are the most beautiful woman in the world."

"I'm your woman," she mumbled between kisses.

He held her away from him. "Say that again?"

"I'm yours."

The irises of his eyes grew dark, like a stormy sky. "Then let me show you how I worship what's mine."

He stripped them both of every stitch then, clearing the way for him to run his tongue across her flesh, from her neck to her breasts. His lavish attention to her nipples had her arching off the bed like a cooncat in the sun.

She couldn't get enough as he moved on—his magical tongue traced its way to her pussy and from there he feasted. There was something about this mating that was so different than all the sex they'd had before, like he was trying to make up for lost time, not just bring her to an orgasming mess. He kept things slow and thorough, no bundle of nerves left unexplored, no part of her not open and available for the taking, including her back entrance. He rubbed a finger all over her pussy, coating it in her arousal, then placed the digit at her pucker.

"Be a good girl, and let me in."

That was all it took, those few words, and she relaxed under this new intrusion. Paired with his tongue at her clit and two other fingers stuck deep in her pussy, she choked on a scream as the orgasm was fast and furious. He'd done this to her, knew how to bring her ultimate pleasure and as she came down from the release, he readied to enter her with his cock.

She moaned out a breathy, "Yes."

Because she wanted to be filled with him. This night would be one she'd remember forever. He'd ruined her for other men and hadn't even found his own release. When he did invade her, it was slow and ground-shattering. She shivered with each movement as he'd enter and pull out. He honed and refined her like a mechanic building a racer. He had already broken any emotional barriers she'd put up. Now he redefined what she'd come to know as lovemaking. They weren't fucking here — this wasn't a simple desire to slack lust, but something more shaping.

After this, she'd never be able to be without him, at least not for too long. Her heart belonged to him, and she sensed the same for his. He leaned down and kissed her.

"If you're mine, then I'm yours. Now will you come around my cock and milk it dry?"

Again, with the commanding words, but that low voice and how he plunged in deep, arching his body in a way that hit the right spot within her… She had no choice but to come. Over and over, the sensations wracked her body and his as well. He froze above her, jerking in small movements that matched her own as they gave away to a release that seemed to go on and on.

When those large tremors subsided and reduced to smaller ones, she wrapped her arms around his shoulders and pulled him to her. The weight of his body satisfied a need for nearness, while his softening cock remained inside her. She felt closest to him in this position and he was surrounding her in the best of ways.

"I'm not hurting you, am I?"

She paused in response, just enjoying the feel of him, processing how whatever minor discomfort she experienced in this moment was nothing compared to what they'd suffered over the last twelve years apart.

"No, you're loving me."

* * * *

When Bridget opened her eyes, Drag was the one sitting in the chair. He was fully clothed and had laid out a shirt and pants for her as well.

"Gina brought those over at my request." He motioned toward the tan pants and the brown T-shirt. "It's not much, but I figured it would give you something clean to wear. Sorry for tearing your shirt."

"It's fine. Tea?"

"Over there." He pointed at the nightstand. "It's not anything fancy like I'm sure you're used to getting. In fact, I wouldn't even call it tea. Gaia brews it, but I don't bother to ask where she gets her leaves." He was somber and a little distant, more than she expected after their early morning lovemaking.

The sun was up. She could tell by the little rays trying to peek into the room through corners where the curtain didn't cover the window. She hadn't paid much attention to the windows, but he had at least three in this room alone. *A lot of exposure.*

"And why are you in a chair and not next to me?"

He sighed and ran a hand over this face. The bandage at his neck was gone—no more wound, just healed skin. He didn't look pale or weakened in any way. Hell, she was tempted to ask him to fuck her again, because whatever this expression was, the one where he wasn't quite looking at her but past her, it had started to spread dread throughout her every limb.

"Because I'm not sure how you're going to react to what I have to say."

She held the mug up close to her mouth so he couldn't see the tremble in her jaw. *No way will I cry, not yet…not until he tells me*. "Then start at the beginning and we'll go from there."

"I couldn't sleep after we…well, you fell asleep, so I got up. I went to the mechanics bay, I sat on the roof, I reviewed the plans and I did everything I could to get a clear head about what comes next."

He went silent and shoved himself out of the chair. His steps reverberated through the floor as he began to pace at the end of the bed. She dared to take a drink then. The bitter yet smooth blend wasn't a tea she was familiar with, but it was refreshing all the same.

"Where we go from here, this next part, we can't do together."

She held her breath, waiting for her chest to seize with that ever-tightening invisible noose that represented how she'd be abandoned yet again after her confession of love and giving everything to him. Had she miscalculated? Her poor heart was still beating, no despair creeping in. In fact, she had expected this because — "You have to race."

"I have to r — you understand?"

"A little, but tell me more." Her mind was wrapping around the concept and her emotional response wasn't as traumatic as she had expected. Somehow her brain had things well under control. She'd been operating in near panic mode for so long that this concept of being honest through discussion had taken her by surprise.

"Well, I'm responsible for these people, this town, and I have to do what's right for them. I can't put one person over their entire wellbeing. After everything that happened with Hemi, the racers, and even this bullshit Moag pulled, if I don't step up and act as their hero now, I'm nothing. I couldn't save you back then, but this time it's different. We're not courting any sponsor, but specific ones. I have to fight that battle. But yours is a different one."

Which made sense. The town still needed to survive and the way to do that was through winning the race. Even if they did prove Moag had stopped the appeal somehow, it would still be a while before anything could be fixed. There would be another filing, appearances, and all of it would take too long. All of Drag's work and the knowledge they'd used to help the Full Throttle gang be more self-sustaining would be wasted without backing. The truth was a gang would never survive without ship contracts, not long term.

"I understand you have to do what's best for them, and I get it. My issue with Cheatham won't be resolved on a race track. I have to face him. I created the monster — it's my job to shove him back down where he belongs. I can be more than the mistakes of past."

He came to her side then, removed the mug from her hands and set it on the bedside table. "You already are. Oh damn, Bridget, those were the scariest words I've ever had to speak."

"Figured I'd leave, right?"

He nodded as he planted his head on her chest. She ran her fingers through his hair, loving how this was where they were. They'd come so far, even though they were both still damaged.

"To be honest, I thought I might, but then I realized what you said made sense. If I take my feelings out of it, we need to handle our responsibilities and after that…if we can take back what we deserve, then maybe—"

"No maybe. We will be together. We'll find a way. But for right now, we do what we need to."

Those words were spoken with such determination that she squeezed him a bit tighter as if holding onto him could somehow infuse his confidence within her. Because soon she'd have to leave, but in the meantime…

"Then I better get out of this bed and go talk to Gina. It's time to find out what she's learned."

Chapter Seventeen

"Outside of the day we came to rescue Jack, I've never been to Macintosh. This gang is about the same size as Full Throttle, but your setup puts your house in the center of town." Gina spoke as she, Gaia and Bridget sat around Bridget's kitchen table with holo-tablets in front of them and a few papers.

The experience of having these two women in her house was equal parts fascinating and weird. Bridget had grown up mostly around men, with very few women wanting to spend time with her because she had been treated as someone above everyone else in the gang. Her status as daughter of the leader had kept them away. Her friends had been the men these two women were around all the time.

"Well, we've got a long way to go. Nothing compared to what you have in Frog Lick."

"Quit downplaying," Gaia whispered. "You act as if your leadership over the last twelve years hasn't been a success."

Had it? Bridget hadn't found the evidence to support Gaia's statement. Not by a long shot. Sure, they had contracts, from Cheatham. Food, from Cheatham. Limited medicine, supplies…all of these damn things came from that bastard.

"We're reduced to the charity of a sponsor. That's not much of a success."

"Success is a subjective term that means different things for each person. But for those on the outside looking in, your time in the leadership position has been a triumph." Gina pressed a button on the holo-tablet and an image appeared on the one in front of Bridget.

The image was of her town, mapped, and the plans for airponics bay and the hydroponics. They weren't just here to help her plot Cheatham's expulsion as her gang's sponsor, but to help with other plans of expansion.

Gina had already shared the truth of what she'd discovered in those papers. The documents had been returned a day prior to Bridget running back to Drag. They were in position, but not entirely. And even though Drag expected her to solve this issue herself, he had refused to let her go alone. Hence why she was flanked by two women he trusted to help keep her safe, in case Cheatham tried anything he'd threatened her with.

Her sponsor hadn't poked his nose around yet, but he would soon enough. They'd arrived late the evening prior. The race was less than a day away.

"Gina's correct. Though your people have faced challenges — all gangs do — the bulk have survived with the circumstances they were given. You've kept them free from turf wars, infighting and from what I can tell, while some may grumble, you've maintained a sponsor. For those who complain, having one does you a great favor."

"That won't be the case after tomorrow."

Gaia reached out and spread a hand over Bridget's. This woman with her pale blonde braids, creamy skin and coffee-colored eyes offered comfort to someone she didn't even know. "Leave that problem for the next leader."

Before Bridget could even ask what she was talking about, Cheatham barged into her house, pulling back the entrance tarp like he had every right to waltz in.

"Where is Trio? I've asked everyone, been to their quarters. I sent them to retrieve you, and you come back with uninvited guests, but not my assassin."

Bridget rose from her chair and approached the piece of shit she'd soon be rid of. He wore a new set of deep purple and red robes, covering most of him. He even had a hood to protect from the sun. But the robes didn't hide the contempt in his eyes or the flush to his cheeks that spoke of too much alcohol consumption.

"I don't know. I returned with the ladies I needed to help me plan my wedding to you."

"We'll be married off world."

Bridget stomped the floor with one foot. "Like hell we will. We marry before I depart in front of these people, out of respect. Following the announcement of whoever you've selected as leader. As for our assassin...they didn't return with me. I didn't question them as I know you have other duties for them to perform."

Cheatham worked his jaw and lips in displeasure. "That damn Inccukai. There was no other job."

The mutterings continued until Cheatham realized what her words declared. The frustration gave way to a smarmy smile. "Fine. A wedding here, but tomorrow evening. I won't prolong this anymore. I'm glad you've come to your senses and decided to honor our agreement."

"You'll let the race proceed?" Her biggest reason for returning was also to ensure he didn't interfere with the championship tomorrow. Drag had to race — that was the one thing he'd proclaimed to her. She believed he would win and after everything she'd done before now, she owed that much to the people of Frog Lick. They deserved a victory.

"I see no reason to interfere. I'm getting what I want, and you're done with that trashy excuse for a gang leader. He really is quite insulting. Even if they win, I doubt sponsors will want to engage with someone so off-putting."

"My father was willing to negotiate with you." She couldn't help it, as much as she wanted to behave and play her role. Cheatham deserved far more than scathing words and retorts, but this was all she could deliver.

The scowl he gave her in response was somewhat rewarding. "You'll be mindful that I won't tolerate that kind of talk once you're my wife. I'll be free to punish you and you'll learn what happens when you disobey. Until then, I'll take solace in the fact you won't be with him. Carry on."

He turned and left the way he had come, his head held high and a smile on his face. No doubt he'd start spreading the word as soon as he left here. By nightfall the entire gang would be wondering what was happening.

"You're going to have a crowd gathering within the next couple hours. What do you want to do?" Gaia had approached on her left side.

"We let them believe Drag has withdrawn his proposal. That's it, right? All we can do now that we're playing this out. I'm done with him. The leader of Full Throttle is my fiancé no more."

Lies, because she'd never be finished. That man was the sole person who could inspire and bring her to sexual satisfaction. He was slowly rebuilding the bonds that had tied them close together and she needed to see what would happen if they could forge a future together.

Everything in her craved what being together could offer. But what would she give up for him?

Chapter Eighteen

"Drag, get your ass out here." Snapper's voice echoed through the mechanics bay and into the small office that Snapper called his. Drag was still there, sitting in the rickety roller chair, looking over the racetrack papers one more time.

He needed the track blueprints embedded in his mind to the point he could see the layout with his eyes closed. Every championship, hell, every race, the commission altered the track and the challenges presented. The track was designed to make the race more exciting than chasing cars in a circle. From rising platforms to different terrains, and even floating obstacles, Drag had to be ready for all the possibilities. Gina had been correct about the possibilities being narrower based on her algorithms, though the number remained over forty. Forty different scenarios he could find himself in. He had to be ready to counter each and every one.

"Hey," Snapper called out from the doorway. "You can't look at that shit all night. You'll go cross-eyed and be useless to us tomorrow. Get out here. I've got the table set up and the sleeping pallets. We're in for a guys-only night. Never thought I'd hear myself say that again."

Drag chuckled as he scooped all the papers into a pile. "You're missing your wife."

"Yeah, I'm not used to her being so far away and I won't lie I was pissed when you asked her to go before asking me."

"It wasn't your choice to make."

Snapper scuffed the sole of his boot against the packed dirt floor. "You're right, but damn if I don't worry."

"I get that." Drag stood up and moved out from behind the desk. "I wouldn't have sent her if I didn't think she'd come back in one piece."

When he caught up to Snapper, they both filed out of the room and into the main area of the mechanics bay. Tonight they would spend the evening with the racer, ensuring its safety. The damn thing wouldn't be left alone until Drag sat in the driver's seat and took off under the green flag.

"What the hell did you manage to pull together with Gaia being gone?"

"Jack took care of the meat, found a couple of fur-buns. Three to be exact and he's already skinned and roasted them," Snapper said as they approached the racer.

The hint of charred flesh hit Drag's nostrils. "I can tell. He may have overcooked them."

"Hey, don't disparage my cooking. Shannon loves my charred fur-bun. We've enjoyed several of them on our overnight trips."

Drag took a seat at the four-sided table Snapper had propped up. There were mugs filled with ale, recycle containers and several other dishes with questionable items. "Vegetables, all raw… You two are hopeless."

"Hey, I can grill those, too."

Snapper shook his head and held out his hands to protect the food on the table. "No, Jack. I think I can only hand one burned part of a meal. I'm no expert, but the veggies were doused in a vinegar mixture. Rune and Gaia call it pickling. I'm willing to give it a try if you are."

"Fine. Then let's dig in."

The three of them filled their plates and their bellies. The char on the fur-bun made the damn thing far tastier than if it had been boiled. The pickled vegetables held a tang and a unique spice that offset the other parts of the meal. There was bread too, a good loaf that they tore bits and pieces from. By the time they had finished, nothing remained.

Jack let out a belch, followed by Snapper, and of course Drag refused to let them win.

"Our fearless leader, always up for a good belch contest."

Drag laughed and the other two joined in. This was what he'd missed over the last couple months. They'd been so busy fighting against all the obstacles that for the first time he felt relaxed. After tomorrow, he wasn't sure where the future would take them all, but he'd ensure the safety and prosperity of Full Throttle.

"When you're a kid, things are simpler."

Snapper scoffed. "Really? That's some weird musing. You thinking about having a kid?"

"Hell, no! Just remembering the days when burping contests and chasing each other around were the activities that kept us busy. Now it's all serious bullshit."

Those thoughts brought back the memories of Bridget. How she used to be the one trailing after them, trying to force herself into their little group of two because she hated being alone. The other girls her age were jealous, the boys... Well, her father didn't trust them. But for reasons that didn't make sense until later, Travis had trusted Snapper.

"No, you're remembering our youth, which is a place I try not to linger on. We had different experiences and while most of them weren't bad, being a secret of my father's wasn't kind toward me," Snapper said.

They all got a little quiet then. Jack had heard some of this but not everything and Drag didn't like airing all their private details so easily. But then again, he'd trust Jack to save his life, so why not with all the stories of their past?

"You know she regrets what she did."

Snapper huffed. "Then she can tell me herself. She never needed you to defend or protect her."

The sentence stung, like being slapped in the face. He'd always possessed an innate desire to offer Bridget extra care and speak up on her behalf if anyone maligned her actions. Those traits told him he'd loved her even back then, admiring first her tenacity, then her sheer strength.

"Maybe not, but I'm willing to give it. The same way you'd do anything for Gina or how Jack would lay down for Shannon."

"You're forgetting that I did," Jack added. "We'd do a lot for the people we love."

Snapper sighed this time. "Damn it, Drag. That's what I was worried about. You falling for her all over again. And you don't think this is going to end badly?"

"Can't help what I feel, the same way you can't." He stared at the table filled with empty plates and dishes of the meal they'd devoured. "She's always been a part of me, even as I tried to cut her out. Hearing what happened back then, knowing the truth... I see where I could have done things a bit different and maybe we would've worked out. But I can't regret what I've gained since we left. Maybe Bridget and I needed the time apart. We needed to grow."

Snapper shoved out of his chair and paced for a minute, muttering to himself before speaking loud enough so Drag could hear. "She came running when her back was against the wall, and you think that's changing. I just...I'm not mad at her for killing the old man. In ways I hated him more than she ever could. Her trying to murder me makes sense. I'm upset because she never bothered to try and talk to me. Never offered me a sibling relationship even though we were side-by-side all those years. Then she tore you up and spit you out." He paused and came around the table, standing in front of Drag, his cybernetic hand extended. "Drag, you're more of a brother to me than anyone. If something happens to you, it would be like losing the only family I've known since birth."

Drag slapped Snapper's hand with his own and stood. "Brother, the one thing you're going to lose is the right to call yourself the best mechanic in Frog Lick. Your wife is moving to take over the top spot."

"You're a bastard," Snapper said, clapping him on the shoulder.

They released each other to find Jack holding two bottles of amber liquid up in the air. "Who's ready for stargazing and a little drinking on the roof?"

"Lead the damn way."

Of course, booze was probably a bad thing at the moment, given where Drag's melancholy musings had wandered to. What Snapper had said, and the phrase about how Bridget didn't need him, still hurt. The more he swigged at the whiskey bottle, the fire from the drink winding its way through him and lingering in his belly, the more he felt guilty.

"You say I didn't need to protect her, but I should have. She had no one, Snapper. After we turned our backs on her, she was alone. I should have stayed, should've tried. I abandoned her and I feel bad for that. I couldn't even protect her the other night from that mummy assassin. If not for Lee…"

Snapper scoffed as he took another swig and passed the bottle to Jack. "The fuck you say. Quit blaming yourself. You're a sludge sack sitting here whining. We can't change what happened then. We can only affect tomorrow. You're the damn one who's always telling me that. The one who encouraged me to go after Gina in the first place. So don't try to talk yourself out of things now. You know who you are, Dakota Michelson. Be that person."

Jack chuckled. "Your name is Dakota?"

"Shut the fuck up," Snapper replied, giving Jack a decent shove to the shoulders. "His birth name is irrelevant but I used it to get a point across."

"Still that's a damn funny name." Their idiot friend was laughing so hard now he'd fallen backward and Snapper rescued the bottle from Jack in time.

"Laugh all you want. I know it's ridiculous. That's why I go by Drag." That and the fact Snapper had said he was always dragging him along with him everywhere. The moniker had stuck. The same way Snapper was called that for always being too sharp in his responses.

"Anyway, before this space hole lost his mind, I was trying to say you should stop being upset at yourself, stop fearing whatever may or may not happen and go for the future you want. You're not beholden to anything or anyone. You love her, then find a way to be with her and don't let anything stop you."

The words were a revelation and rejuvenating, unlike the comments before. Drag mused a bit as he nursed what remained of one of the bottles. The stars twinkled above them. Maybe after tomorrow he could focus less on what he thought he should do and worry a little more about what he wanted.

"You agree with all those words you just puked out?" he couldn't help but ask, as Jack got a hold of himself and sat back up straight.

Snapper shook his head. "Hell no, but it's what you need to hear. That's what matters. The same way you once told me to quit living in the past and go after the damn girl."

"I think I said things a bit different."

Snapper shoved into him. "Yeah, but the message was the same."

That message being Drag needed to get his shit together and follow his own heart—but not until after the race.

"Think it's time we got back downstairs and slept. I'm going to be useless if I finish off this bottle."

Jack held out his hands. "Well, I won't be. Besides, you two asses snore and if I have to trade a night in bed with Shannon to bunk up with you fools, then I'm going to make sure I'm passed the hell out."

Drag started laughing, followed by Snapper. Pretty soon they were all holding their stomachs. The mirth did good to clear away some of the haze from the liquor and let him forget his worries momentarily. Tomorrow everything would change again and Drag hoped he was able to deliver when it counted.

Chapter Nineteen

"Are you good?" Snapper's voice asked through the helmet connection.

Drag took a deep breath as he stared out onto the track. "Yeah, as good as I'll ever be."

They were minutes away from race start. Already Drag had picked up on a few of the track obstacles, ones that Gina had predicted with accuracy. The woman was a blessing to Frog Lick. Drag's racer was lined up next to Skeiron. Damn sharp-toothed fool of a driver with a half-visor was grinning at Drag like an idiot.

"Well, watch out. Skeiron and those Gemino klogs are cheating bastards. No doubt they're packing some sort of trick."

Drag ignored the Skeiron driver. The Gemino racer with the bright green tail fins, on the other hand, was in front of him. "All you need to do is confirm my opening. I get ahead of these fools and I'm in the clear. We've confirmed no one else has mastered the NiteOx."

"Yeah, Gina double-checked. So far no one can replicate what we did, but Singh is getting close."

Gina had built an ingenious engine that provided a power boost with a combustible material called NiteOx. She'd even found a way to ignite it outside the main engine manifold so the specs of the racer still followed the Mars Racing Commission guidelines.

The commission... Hell, that brought him back to Bridget, who was somewhere up there in the boxes above the regular stands. Was she watching him or waging battle on her own? He'd been privy to none of the information since she'd departed for Macintosh with Gina and Gaia. The women had promised to serve as protection for Bridget, along with coming up with a plan for how she would expose Moag.

Was she confronting him right now? Had she gathered other leaders like their friends? He had no way of confirming what was happening and they were minutes, maybe seconds from announcing the race start.

"Has Gina come back yet?" Drag asked.

The mechanic had promised to be in the racing pit with Snapper by the time the start flag was waved.

"No, she's not here, but you agreed to let Bridget take care of herself. Your focus is the race, so stay there."

"Fine...but let me know when she's returned. I'm not going to be able to keep going at one-hundred percent if I'm not sure Bridget is okay."

He couldn't make out Snapper's response because the crowd started to roar and the lights signaling the race start had begun the countdown. Drag saw the flag waver on their perch, high above the crowd, suspended over the track. A scary job, and one Drag would never want, but that waver was smiling and the first flag was held up. This was a black flag, a preparation. The holo-screens projected a countdown. They were at the ten solar second mark.

Whatever was going on with Bridget would need to take a backseat for the moment, so Drag could win. He was determined to get in front. From there it would be smooth sailing.

The yellow flag came next—five seconds to go.

Drag readjusted his grip on the wheel. The engine beneath the hood of the racer rumbled, along with all the others on the track in front, beside and behind him. Two seconds left. The waver held up the green flag, gripping the fabric with one hand and the rod with the other.

Then it flew and the scent of burned rubber filled the air along with the screech of tires as each racer peeled out on the track. It was time.

The compression of the accelerator, the revving, the even push on the clutch as Drag shifted through the gears… Mere seconds passed and he was already in gear six. The other racers kept pace with his, though he was starting to see a few of them struggle. For a twenty-lap race, performance was key. If those who were already rattling and rumbling didn't get things under control, they would fail the obstacle laps.

"There's a hole between Gemino and Singh. Just rub 'em," Snapper's voice crackled over the helmet radio.

"Any word?"

"Shit, get ahead of those cars."

Drag did as instructed, bulleting past Skeiron, before maneuvering between Singh and Gemino. Barnabas and Osprerine were the remaining two racers in his way now.

"Tell me more while I wait for the next opening."

Snapper scoffed. "You're so sure there'll be one?"

"Barnabas gets scared every time. You know that from our regional races. If Osprerine rides too close, we'll get our shot. Now where is Gina?"

He was all tension and strength, coiled and in control, though his stomach was a riot of nerves. Not for the race — he could do this blindfolded with as much as he'd studied Gina's predictions and her analysis of the other racers and drivers. The woman had left nothing to chance. But not knowing Bridget's status was killing his soul. He cursed himself for his suggestion they operate separately.

His chest grew tight if he even entertained the hundreds of possibilities. Ratcheting up that anxiety to the speeds of his racer was a damn bad idea. Then he spotted the Osprerine driver moving in close as predicted.

"I think it's time."

"Then make the move," Snapper replied.

Drag moved into position. It was seconds before Barnabas pulled away, leaving enough space for Drag to squeeze his racer through and take the lead spot. Now, he'd wait for Snapper's confirmation to ignite the NiteOx and make the lead impossible for anyone to retake.

"Can I talk to her now?"

Snapper sighed. "Yeah, but be prepared. Those drivers behind you are steamed and they are right on your ass. We're not triggering NiteOx until lap four and you're just coming into the first turn of lap two."

"Yes, mother. Now let me talk to Gina."

There was a bit of static over the helmet comms. Then he could hear her voice. "I'm here Drag. You're doing great, by the way."

"Appreciate the kind words, but you know why you're talking to me. Give me an update."

Gina sighed and Drag didn't like the sound of her exhale at all. "Bridget is fine, a little nervous. Just like a driver before the start of a race."

"And the plan?"

"It's in motion. Though that Moag…he's one to be wary of. We were at Macintosh and I wouldn't be surprised if he had something up his sleeve. He agreed to leave you alone as long as Bridget married him, but that wedding is set for tonight. If she somehow doesn't sway the commission or he convinces them that our evidence is fake… I'm not sure if she'll be able to get rid of him. There are a lot of variables."

He'd entered lap three as Gina finished. One more lap and the NiteOx would be triggered. After that he'd be locked into the rest of the race, not to mention the obstacles would make pit stops impossible. Drivers had five laps to determine if they needed adjustments — the remaining fifteen were dedicated to performing sometimes near-impossible feats.

"You can't tell me you don't have a percentage of success already generated."

"I don't feel like sharing those numbers. You need to focus. We're half a lap away from triggering the engine booster. There's no time to be distracted."

"Then tell me she'll be okay." Drag kept his eyes trained on turn three. When he glanced between his rearview, the Gemino driver was trying to maneuver to overtake him. *Not happening today, you idiot.*

He pressed on the accelerator and sped up a tiny bit, pushing the racer to its max speed capabilities without the NiteOx.

"I'm not going to tell falsehoods and you know that. Just be advised that no matter what happens today, we did try and Bridget knows the risks she's undertaking."

Gina's response did nothing to quell the rising right in his chest and stomach. No way could he lose her. Moag wasn't a fool—he didn't get to the position he was in without suspecting anyone could betray him. Should Drag just let her risk it all alone? He'd told her he needed to put his allegiance with his gang and chosen them over her. *But is that right?*

Snapper told him the previous night to work for the future he wanted. That future was one with Bridget in it, no substitutions. He refused to continue on in a world without her present and by his side.

But getting that future would mean stopping now, not finishing the race and running the risk of Full Throttle going without a sponsor. Could he sacrifice the people he'd promised to represent for the woman he loved?

"We're coming out of turn four. It's time."

No, if Moag did have a plan to keep her under his thumb, if she was forced to be with him and leave Mars... *I'll never make it.* Full Throttle would survive with or without this win. They'd already proven to be more resilient than any other gang on Mars next to those who were unaffiliated. They would suffer no penalties. Those from Full Throttle in attendance would be screaming for his head, almost all of them. He started to decelerate and pull toward the pit lane.

Snapper's voice boomed in his ear. "What the fuck are you doing, Drag? We agreed the flash before the clash. Crinkle before the dinkle. Don't let your cock drive you away from your commitments."

"It's not my dick doing the talking here. It's my heart. I love her, Snapper. More than I care about my future in Full Throttle or the gang itself. May whatever deity ruling over these planets strike me down if that's wrong, but I can't risk losing her. Gina can't tell me a percentage or predict what will happen and that scares the shit out of me."

"They are all pulling ahead. It would take the NiteOx and a miracle just to retake the lead. Drag, don't do this."

He pulled into the pit lane, and let the other racers zoom past him. They did and there were roars of frustration and excitement coming as Skeiron and Gemino battled for lead position. The Full Throttle pit wasn't far now. He'd pull in and head toward Bridget. His whole body shook as he slowed the racer, part from this urgent need to be out of this confined space and the rest a mess of guilt because he'd gone against his own word.

"I have to, Snapper. If I can choose to be a hero for Frog Lick or one for Bridget..." He took a deep breath then slowly exhaled, keeping his gaze on the stopping point ahead of him. "Then I'd rather be a hero for her. I can't lose her again, not this time."

Chapter Twenty

Bridget was all smiles with minutes to go before the race started. She wanted to wrap this mess up within the first five laps so that she'd be able to give her full attention to Drag and watch him win.

Gaia and Gina had already left her. She'd walked into the suite with Cheatham present, along with his ally, Paulos. There were leaders from Osprerine, Zephyr and several others, including a pair of faces she'd never expect to be nice to her.

"You arrived safe and sound. That's good," Hemi said as he outstretched his cybernetic hand to her.

She took the greeting and didn't miss his slightly tighter handshake.

"Don't try to rip her hand off. She's here to do the right thing," said a blonde woman beside him, who Bridget recognized as Sophia—once a daughter of a gang leader like herself and now the co-leader of Aurestral alongside Hemi.

"It's a pleasure to meet you again, though I hope these are better circumstances," Bridget offered, shaking Sophia's hand now.

The other woman took it. "I think they are, or at least we'll find out in a minute. I need to chat with a few more folks before we get started." Sophia nodded and smiled. "We've got your back."

The peace offering buoyed Bridget's spirit as she traversed the room, speaking with other leaders and posing casual inquires if they would give her support after seeing her holo-communication the day prior. Cheatham appeared oblivious, too busy drinking champagne and sharing anecdotes about how he had the best of everything, including the best racers and drivers. If the commission on racing hadn't approved Full Throttle to use their questionable engine, Macintosh would be present on the field.

Bridget did her best not to roll her eyes. While she had faith in the mechanics and drivers from Macintosh, their hearts hadn't been in the race this year and they had easily been pushed back by other teams more devoted to the win. Even if Full Throttle had lost, it would have been near impossible for Macintosh to win today. She felt a bit of relief that they weren't in the race.

"I'm sure they would have performed admirably if Macintosh had qualified. Aah, the race is about to begin. There is the flag waver," Minshe, the Aurora representative, stated. Her long black hair was pulled back into a high ponytail with polished rock clips adorning various sections. Her clothes were mixture of greens and blues that were similar to the style of Sophia's dress. "May I suggest we quiet and pay attention to the festivities about to start?"

A confirmed effort to silence everyone and stop the talking, but for Bridget this was her chance to begin. "Representative Minshe, I was wondering if I might have a word before the race gets underway?"

The older woman glanced over her shoulder at Bridget. "This can't wait?"

"No, I'm afraid not. I'll need Representative Ulys' attention as well." Bridget didn't miss the frown Cheatham cast her way. But Minshe and Ulys—a man dressed in a long gray, white and black tunic with a short mohawk—turned her way.

This is it, no going back now.

"What can we help you with, Macintosh leader?"

Bridget swallowed hard and her words were caught. Did she dare to try? What if everyone around her backed out? It wasn't hard to believe she could be left all alone and abandoned again when trying to stand up to this evil. If she didn't try, that would be even worse. A future with Cheatham would kill her. She refused to let her people suffer, let those on Mars be brought down by this deep-seated corruption that could spread throughout and defeat everything the people of this planet had worked so hard for.

"I want to speak to you about the Wespero representative. It appears there is some corruption amid the commission."

Gasps were heard, though those she'd already talked to were aware. Gina and Gaia had helped Bridget spread the word. Shannon had even gone to Zephyr to deliver the evidence due to their refusal to possess certain technologies.

"This is a serious accusation, Macintosh leader. What proof do you have?"

Cheatham stepped over then. "None whatsoever. Bridget, I urge you to silence yourself."

"She will not." Yenna, the Zephyr leader, with her red and orange mantle, stepped forward then. "I've seen her evidence and it is damning. You, Cheatham, will be silent until all is presented."

The overbearing presence of her sponsor diminished under Yenna's rebuff, though she didn't miss the hatred in his gaze. He was training that view on Bridget as well, along with Sophia and Hemi who'd flanked her left side. With these three beside her, she found the courage to pull the holo-tablet from her jacket.

"If you take a look here, you'll see copies of documents obtained that show where Moag Cheatham used his wealth and status to bribe the Wespero representative, Paulos, on the racing and the shipping commission to revoke Full Throttle's appeal and in addition secure rights for special privileges for Macintosh." Bridget handed the tablet to Minshe's outstretched hands. The woman scrolled through the communications Gina had pieced together and the photos from the security cameras with the secret meetings and a couple transcriptions of conversations even Bridget hadn't realized had taken place after she and Drag had placed the devices.

Paulos, who stood not far from them, was cowering, nibbling on his damn nails and edging toward the door with each second that passed.

"Hemi, can you stop him from leaving?"

The cyborg didn't move, his frown evident as he eyed the Wespero coward.

"Please?" Bridget asked. "I'd be grateful."

That got Hemi moving along with the nudging elbow from his wife. "Fine. Stay still, you bastard. If I have to chase you, I'll get pissed."

Paulos, in his yellow and red flowing robe, let out a yelp and dropped to the floor. "Please don't hurt me. I had no choice. I had to say yes, or he said I'd die."

More shock echoed through the room as the announcement that the race was underway sounded.

"Shut up, you spineless sludge sack!" Cheatham roared, his usual calm, patient façade melting away.

"Protectorate guards, restrain Paulos. We'll do the same to you, Cheatham, if you can't control yourself," Minshe commanded.

The guards, decked in their silver racing-day armor, stepped forward, two from each entrance, and took flanking positions around Paulos, freeing Hemi from any type of commitment. Bridget wanted them to surround Cheatham.

"May I ask, Macintosh leader, why you've brought this information to us? It benefits your gang if you continue your relationship with Cheatham." Ulys asked this of her as he started to look closely at the documents on the tablet that Minshe had handed him.

Bridget shook her head. "No, it doesn't. My people have become too reliant on Cheatham and what he provides. We've lost our way, and they are willing to sacrifice themselves to continue to be hobbled by him. Besides, his brand of business invites more criminals to this planet that would exploit our gangs and way of life for their own benefit. Mars needs to be able to stand on its own. Sponsors should be business partners, not dictators. This man would try to force me to marry him, and would lie and cheat his way to impound or deny any gang that tried to expose him, including me."

The other leaders started to express outrage then, Sophia and Yenna included. As female leaders, their outrage matched hers. *No way can we allow such tyranny to continue.*

"Like my father, who would deal in human trafficking with people like Cheatham and his kind. We can no longer allow this. Commission, you must act." Sophia said all this as she pumped her fist in the air repeatedly. "Speak now, leaders. We demand action."

"Agreed," Yenna joined in. "We were of similar minds once, and we've sacrificed our people time and again in the name of greed. We must learn to do without, to build without. These upper fools who would try to steal from us could do with a little lesson that we won't be their slaves any longer."

Others from Osprerine, and even Singh, started to voice their opposition and disgust. They spit at the guarded Paulos and at Cheatham, who continued to be silent, but his brooding gaze and hunched shoulders told Bridget he wanted to explode.

"Got you." She mouthed the words at him, and he growled in return.

"The commissions will confer, minus the Wespero reps, of course," Minshe called out to the room. All four remaining members gathered in the corner. Though it was unheard of for reps from Aurora and Auster to exclude Wespero's input, this situation was unique. For once the leaders were willing to voice their frustrations at the situation.

The cacophony of dissent continued to grow, unhappy voices in unison with this revelation. The holo-tablet of evidence had been passed now to other leaders and the shipping commission representatives. The Wespero shipping commission rep, Gaunt, had been also thrown in between those four protectorate guards with Paulos.

"This is your damn fault, Paulos. I told you to burn the evidence, not keep it," Gaunt admonished his partner in crime, but they were both suckers, wooed and drawn in by Cheatham's offers.

"I kept those to hold him to his agreements. I did it to keep me safe."

Gaunt roared and shoved at Paulos' hunched body on the floor. "Look where that got us."

The laps were counting down. At least two had passed of the first five, Bridget could tell from a quick glance at the holo-screens outside the viewing window. They were running out of time, and though the debate taking place around her seemed to imply she was winning her own battle here, there was no confirmation.

Not until Cheatham is in chains.

"Silence, everyone!" Minshe called out. "The commissions agree we will replace the Wespero members. Paulos and Gaunt will be tried for treason against the Mars Commission and our laws that representatives remain impartial at all times."

"What about Cheatham?" Sophia asked.

Other voices mimicked the question and Bridget stood a little straighter. She wasn't alone — the leaders here saw the same problems she did. The sponsor's poison couldn't be allowed to spread. For once she found herself in a group of like-minded people. Maybe more faith in the future of Mars was due. Seemed folks weren't as committed to the same old philosophies as previous leaders had been.

"We have no authority to charge him as he's not a resident of Mars," Ulys offered. The other commission reps agreed.

Minshe raised her hands to quell the outrage of a response. "But we do believe he should be expelled from our planet and not permitted to be a sponsor any longer. His business with our planet and the gangs will be banned."

"Now, wait a minute," Cheatham said. His response sounded half between an engine bellows and the blowback from a bad fuel mix. "I deserve a chance to defend my actions. I acted in the best interests —"

"There's been an accident on the track. A racer collided with a wall. I think it may be on fire," the Singh leader announced to the room. A bright flashing light blinked multiple times on the holo-screens for a race pause. The fifth lap was almost over.

Bridget's heart leaped into her throat. What if Drag had crashed? No, he wouldn't. His racer was superior...unless Cheatham hadn't kept his word. Fear was like a rainstorm on the plains of Auster, sharp and deadly with ice crystals, paining her skin. Every part of her wanted to run to the window, but there were people in the way.

"Hold, leaders, don't be distracted. Let's resolve this so our attention can go toward the race." The words from Minshe fell on deaf ears as the various leaders present and even a couple of the protectorate guards were stepping toward the viewing window. Did she dare to look?

Or do I just go?

"Bridget, I think it's Drag," Hemi called out over the crowd and those words were enough to get her feet moving.

Chapter Twenty-One

Bridget was out through the door, even with various objections shouted in her direction as she ran. She had to ensure Drag was okay. As she ran a short way down the open hallway, no one was paying attention to her. All eyes were on the track, on the racer that was aflame.

Please don't let it be him.

She reached the nearest staircase and started her descent. It would take her at least five minutes to get to the pits and by then it could be too late. The stairwell was cut off from everything so there was no way to check the progress of the race. She kept her focus on the stairs beneath her feet.

Her skin crawled with panic, as if a part of her would jump forth if able and take off running even faster. But she was limited by being a mere human. Four flights of stairs separated her from the door that would lead to the tunnel taking her under the track and to the pit areas for the racers.

Each step seemed to produce an echo around her. Then she paused, waiting to hear the slamming of feet against the stairs. Those climbing steps didn't belong to her and were coming from below. She glanced over the railing and saw a flash of silver.

"Drag?"

"Bridget!" His voice reverberated off the walls up to her. Her heart slammed in her chest, then regained its racing pitter-patter as she started to run and half-jump as many steps as she could. She rounded the corner of a flight and slammed into this chest.

His arms came to grip hers. "Are you okay? Is everything all right? How did you escape?"

Bridget struggled against him and thrashed her arms with limited movement. "Why are you asking me those questions? What about you? The racer is on fire!"

They both paused and looked in each other's eyes. The stormy blue of Drag's gaze stilled her. He looked wild and desperate, his chest heaving as he panted. They'd been running toward each other.

"Why are you here?" she found herself asking as she stopped fighting against him and wrapped her palms around his forearms as tight as he held her.

"You first?"

"I was coming to find you. I heard about the fire and thought the worst, that Cheatham had gone back on his word."

"He did, but that doesn't matter."

"What?" Her question came out as a screech even as Drag smothered the noise with a kiss. She melted against him then, letting his tongue meld with hers. Their connection was as strong as ever. He smelled of rubber, dirt and smoke. The fire had touched him.

I'll kill that bastard myself.

When he ended the kiss, he muttered against her lips, "I love you. I was coming to you. There might have been something set on the pit track. I rolled over something and it stuck to the tires. It would have ignited any racer on the lane, just took a bit longer than Cheatham planned. Maybe he hoped... I don't know, don't care. I was out of the racer before it caught fire. Had to come find you, make sure you were safe."

Bridget shook her head even as her heartbeat still pounded in her ears and she kept adjusting her grip on his arms, desperately trying to ensure this was real. Had he walked away from the race for her? "Why are you sacrificing Full Throttle's chance at a win?"

"Because I lied. That doesn't matter to me as much as you do. Forget winning and sponsors—I want a future for me and there isn't one where I'm happy unless you're part of it."

She couldn't breathe for a minute. This was all her dreams coming true. To be chosen, to be loved so much the person would be willing to let everything go for her. "Say that again."

"I should have told you how much I loved you before, back then. I want love more than anything. It means more than power, being a leader, winning, everything. I'm willing to give you my heart and the chance to pulverize it into a million pieces if you decide to. I didn't say it enough, just took for granted what we had, but Bridget... I fucking love you. More than anything else this world or universe can offer."

She kissed him then, doing her best to show him how much those words meant. The power they gave her, the strength and belief that no matter what happened upstairs now or on the track, they'd be together. Forget their gangs, their obligations...all that mattered was them together and the future would be bright.

Bridget was so lost in her moment with Drag that she barely heard the slamming of doors and the heavy footsteps on the stairs. She didn't care who it was coming up behind them. They could keep moving. She'd be tempted to get naked right here, just to show Drag how much he meant to her. How their bond transcended all else.

"I love you, too," she said between kisses. She released her hold on his forearms and trailed her hands up to wrap them around his neck. "Just promise me you won't leave me again."

"I won't," he murmured, eyes closed as he nipped at her lips.

Then as fast as they'd connected, she was ripped from him. The breath whooshed out of her as her back collided with the wall. Cheatham's roar echoed around them.

"I think it's the opposite. You'll be leaving him. You belong to me. We agreed."

Drag shoved at Cheatham, and the sponsor fell backward on the steps. "Don't think so. She lied—we were never apart and she doesn't want to go with you. So back up."

He crossed over to her, and Bridget tried her best to get her bearings, but her wrist hurt and she was pretty sure the fall into the wall had bruised a couple ribs. Breathing came with pain.

"You bastard, you're so desperate now. The commission already agreed that you're done here. I'm not obligated to honor any deal or bargain. You've lost your control here." She managed those words even between winces as Drag helped her to a standing position.

"Are you all right?" he asked, his concern for her so damn sweet she admired him even more.

"I'll be better once we get away from this space hole."

Chatham's gaze moved farther down the flight stairs, and he chuckled. "You finally showed up. I've been waiting for you. Take care of these two, however you want. But I want their heads. I'll mount them to the front of my ship so these Mars morons can see what I do to people who cross me."

Those words got Bridget looking and her body tensed with fresh spasms of pain from her ribcage. The Inccukai was standing there, covered in their wrappings and those eyes. *Didn't Lee kill this creature?*

"So much for having the upper hand," Bridget murmured. She leaned against Drag, soaking in the heat from his body. At least if she was killed, she'd be by his side. This time they would fall together, instead of apart. Whatever happened now, she was able to leave this world knowing how much he cared for her, how her own feelings had been returned.

The Inccukai approached in slow measured steps, as if they were a reaper of death from the old Earth tales her father had told, though instead of coming for Drag and Bridget, the assassin headed for Cheatham. Drag wasn't gripping her tight. No, he was smiling.

The hood came down, and a long, black ponytail was visible. "Afraid I don't take orders from you, Moag Cheatham. Toni sends her regards and you're right. No one gets away once they cross the Morales family." Lee's voice was crystal clear as the woman removed two knives.

The man who'd plagued her for the last twelve years was scrambling up the steps, crawling with his hands and feet. The first of the knives flew, landing in one of Cheatham's palms, followed by the next. Screams of anguish and fear emerged from his throat. The bravado and cockiness that this man had always exuded disappeared.

Bridget was frozen, locked in place, watching in half-horror and half-relish as her tormentor was punished. He stopped moving and turned to begging.

"Please, I'll give the flash back and the tech I promised to deliver. I wouldn't go back on a deal. I was delayed."

Lee never wavered, her pursuit steady and fierce as a glimmer reflected off the tip of one of her blades. "Afraid it's too late for that. They want proof you're no longer a problem and won't take advantage of anyone else."

"No, I don't deserve this."

"You deserve even less," Bridget whispered under her breath as Lee slit Cheatham's throat, then, with the same blade, she neatly sliced off one of his fingers. The gurgling sounds were all Bridget heard as he tried to clutch at the open wound and stabbed himself instead with the tips of the blades poking through the center of his palms. The amount of blood spreading down the steps was horrifying.

But no more than what he deserved as she recalled the same noises her father had made the night Cheatham had watched her kill Travis Macintosh. This was a revenge of the sweetest kind.

Lee stepped back, leaping out of the path of those fluids, and used Trio's robe to soak up the blood in her path. "My job is done. Justice is served. Would you agree, Drag?"

"I would. Thank you for your help."

"Not a problem. He'd already made too many enemies, and that piece of crap who worked for him was one who deserved far more punishment than I gave. They killed too many I cared about over the years. Gina did me a favor calling Toni and Emilio."

Wait, what? There were questions, but Bridget found they might be better kept for a private conversation between her and Drag. Gina had somehow orchestrated this, and that scared the crap out of Bridget. The woman was inhuman in some of the ways her mind worked. Bridget couldn't comprehend the relief flooding her body. There was no more Cheatham, no more threats, except... "How do we explain this?"

"I wouldn't stick around," Lee said. "While you wouldn't be punished per se, probably not a good idea to be tied to this. With that, I'll make my own exit. Good luck and consider the Morales' debt to Full Throttle paid."

Lee pointed to Drag, and he nodded before she jumped over the railing and disappeared.

"That woman. Who is she?"

"Someone you never want as an enemy. Let's just say the people she works for owed me."

"Morales...any ties to Gina?"

Drag shrugged. "Afraid I can't answer that, but you care to take her advice and get out of here?"

Bridget put her hand in his. "I don't think I can run."

The remark got her lifted up into Drag's arms as carefully as he could, though she still hissed at the sharp pain in her side.

"Then I'll carry you."

"How long will you take care of me like this? Protecting me, killing my oppressors... You're my hero, Drag." She pressed a soft kiss to his lips as he touched his forehead to hers. This...she'd give up everything to forever have this. That was what she was willing to surrender. In that moment, with the scent of blood and death around them, she prepared to say farewell to the life she'd lived.

"For as long as you'll let me."

Chapter Twenty-Two

"I'm not ready for this," Snapper said as he looked at his reflection in the mirror. Gone was his usual mechanics uniform replaced with a tight-knit shirt of dark green and khaki-colored pants and grav boots. His hair was slicked back. Gina had even trimmed his facial hair down to nothing but the goatee.

Gina wrapped her arms around his shoulders, the pale color of her forearms a sharp contrast against his skin. Her purple gaze locked on his in the mirror. "No one is ever ready to assume the mantle of leadership, but you deserve this. The people chose you. They had other options."

Yes, they did. In the weeks since the championship race, where Gemino had won and the murder of the treacherous sponsor, Moag Cheatham, had taken place, the gangs of Wespero had been thrown into disarray, from nominations of new commission representatives to the fact that Macintosh and Full Throttle gangs were faced with appointing new leaders as Bridget and Drag had disappeared following the race.

Snapper smiled. "I never thought I'd be back here."

"Does it feel good to be home?" Gina stepped back and Snapper turned to face her.

The emotions within him had his hands a bit shaky. It had been more than twelve years since they had fled in the middle of the night. Macintosh had welcomed him back with open arms, voting to appoint him leader.

All he had to do was step outside that door and claim his spot.

"Do you think Gaia is nervous today?"

Gina nodded her head. "I would think so. You both have big shoes to feel, I believe the phrase says."

"It's fill, not feel. I'm thankful you're by my side. We can do this."

She extended her hand, and he took it, feeling the strength from her radiating into him. This was his future—no more hiding in a mechanics garage. He would have never thought to step up if not for Drag and for Bridget's letter. When his sister returned, he would have a lot to say to her, but for now... *Time to take charge of my future.*

They both walked out of the leader's house to roars of joy from the gathered gang. Full Throttle wouldn't be present today, but a shared alliance celebration would be forthcoming.

"All cheer our new leader, Snapper."

Macintosh and Full Throttle would never be the same, and for once Snapper was okay with the changes to come.

* * * *

Under the cover of hoods and sun goggles, Drag stood beside Bridget and watched as Snapper and Gina emerged to cheers. Bridget squeezed his arm, and he glimpsed a tear track on her cheek.

"Everything is how it should be now," he whispered in her ear as he hugged her close.

She winced. "Not too tight."

She was still recovering from the fractured ribs Cheatham had given her. While almost healed, she had to take it easy and Drag did his best to care for her. But with all the excitement of the impending appointment days, she'd refused to enjoy their refuge and wanted to attend the ceremonies.

"If only for a minute," she'd begged and Drag could never deny her anything.

"Have you seen enough?" he asked as they continued to watch the procession of Snapper and Gina shaking hands, the drinks being passed and the start of a party that would last well into the night and beyond.

"Yes, let's return to Frog Lick, for Gaia."

They slipped away, back to their hauler, filled with their supplies—all courtesy of Rune and Jack who'd helped them pack in the hours when they'd left the racing track and returned to Frog Lick following Cheatham's death.

Since then, they'd traveled, together, sleeping where they wanted to, camping and exploring the wilds between the gangs across all three territories, but never too far from home. They planned to venture to Aurora next, and Aurestral where Hemi and Sophia wanted them to visit.

But they couldn't depart just yet. The hours' long drive to Frog Lick showed the slow setting of the sun, and when they arrived, the appointment ceremony was already over and had given way to the party. Music and singing voices roared from the Watering Hole, though the crowd had also spilled into the street. That was where he found his brother and Petal.

"Ahoy, Drag and Bridget. You're a little late. The appointment was announced midday, but we're glad you came."

Drag hopped out of the hauler and embraced Rune in a tight hug. This was what he missed most. Though being with Bridget brought pleasure each day, he still pined for those he cared about. Change meant saying goodbye to things he'd once believed would always exist. "How are you, brother?"

"Better than ever. What's to come, the alliance with Macintosh, the future is bright. And Petal's pregnant."

Bridget let out a gasp. "My gods, really?"

She and Petal shared a gentle embrace. New life, new possibilities. This was the future Drag had been fighting for, and now stepping aside brought even more joy.

"Yes, we are ready," Rune replied. "This has been a long time coming and I think we're safe enough to bring a child to this world."

Drag clapped Rune on the back. "Congratulations, brother. To a successful birth and another brilliant mind to further Full Throttle's success."

Gaia stepped out then, with Jack and Shannon flanking her. She waved and Drag dared a wave back. Like the letter Bridget had written for Snapper, he'd left a message for Gaia. The time had come for new leadership, and it wasn't a cyborg who should be in charge.

The pale blonde woman with her swinging braids marched toward him. "You're late."

"As I see it, right on time. Better I show up after you were appointed so no one would think I wanted the spot back. You're not going to hit me, are you?"

Gaia shook her head, her fists at her side relaxing. "No, as much as I want to… I needed this, the push. I'm ready and I thank you for believing in me. I assume Petal and Rune shared the good news."

"I'm going to be an uncle," Drag replied even as his eyes gathered tears. Bridget was by his side as if he'd psychically called for her, supporting him even with her own aches and pains.

"Love, seen enough?"

This part hurt…leaving everything they had built. She understood how he felt, the tearing at his gut as he stared at the buildings that had supported him through his darkest times and the people who'd been there when Bridget couldn't be.

"Yeah, it's time."

"You'll come back for the birth, right?" Rune asked.

Drag nodded as he swiped at his eyes. Silly tears sprouting at the wrong times. "Send the message. Jack and Gina will know how to reach us."

"I sure will," Jack called out from the Watering Hole porch. "Take care of him."

This was directed at Bridget, who nodded and replied, "Always."

They made it back to the hauler with a few more farewells, then they zipped off into the night. Bridget rested in the passenger seat as Drag drove. The stars twinkled above them, and the air had already gotten cooler.

"We travel until the moon rises high—that all right?" he asked.

"Yes. As long as I'm with you, I'm up for anything."

He'd depend on those words for the rest of his life—together forever, with whatever tomorrow brought their way.

Glossary

Airponics: Indoor greenhouse.

APU: Abbreviation for Allied Planetary Union, the governing body of all the planets in the Milky Way, except Earth, Earth's moon and Mars.

Aurestral: Affiliated Aurora territory gang-town.

Aurora: One of the three territories on Mars.

Auster: One of the three territories on Mars.

Barnabas: Affiliated Wespero territory gang-town.

BCS: Body Collection Service, an organization founded by the APU that collects dead bodies for bone harvesting.

Bob-tailed scratcher: Possum-type animal with claws and bobbed tail.

Bone powder: Used to power the slip drive by mixing with water. Made from human bones. Most potent when mixed with urine as the acid mixes with the carbon molecules that light up more with electricity.

Bootleggers: Smugglers who run illegal booze from Earth to other planets.

Bumdum: Slang term for bummer.

Coon cat: Striped feral cat with a bushy tail.

Crinkle: Slang term for money.

Dust honey: Slang term for an attractive woman who lives on Mars and hangs around guys or gals in the hopes of gaining attention, money or notoriety.

Fatch: Alternative to the word fuck, in regional use by those from the Upper planets. Used alone or as a noun or verb in various phrases to express annoyance, contempt or impatience.

Flash: Slang term for money.

Fur-buns: Rabbit-type animal that lives in the wilds of Mars.

Gold leaves: Monetary currency, pressed gold in sheets as thin as leaves. Folks call it crinkle or flash depending on who they are and where they're from.

Goosemert: Mouse-like animal that burrows and lets out a honking wail.

Grav boots: Boots with a gravity lock built into the soles, designed for those who travel in space and may need to spacewalk.

Haulers: Four-seater coverless vehicles with a bed attached for hauling supplies or parts.

Holo-communicator: Handheld device used for talking to others, which can also project a 3D image of their face, if desired.

Holo-tablets: Handheld computers that can project images into the air in a 3D format.

Hover cycle: Motorcycle that hovers instead of having the wheels touching the ground.

Hydroponics: Water-processing plant.

Inccukai: Elite assassins that were raised and trained to protect APU Ambassadors. Some have left the order and taken jobs as freelance bodyguards and mercenaries. Often get their bodies enhanced with tech.

Joseph's balls: Curse slang term frequently used on the Lower Planets.

Klogs: People who lie about who they really are.

Kuargen: Affiliated Wespero territory gang-town.

Lower Planets: Earth and Mars.

Macintosh: Affiliated Wespero territory gang-town.

Marsanium: Iron-based ore mined on Mars and used to build ships.

Mars Racing Commission: Oversight committee that approves and monitors all racing activities on Mars.

Mars Shipping Commission: Oversight committee that approves and monitors all shipbuilding and mining activities on Mars.

Moonie: Slang term for those who live on Earth's moon.

MP: Mars Protectorate.

NiteOx: Deadly fuel-enhancing gas discovered in 2330.

Nkosi: Affiliated Wespero territory gang-town.

Osprerine: Affiliated Auster territory gang-town.

Recycle: Waste water processed and filtered for human consumption, but not as high quality as pure water.

Rising Sun: Affiliated Wespero territory gang-town.

Runners: Smugglers who run illegal drugs from Earth to other planets.

Scurdy: Scaredy-cat, someone who is afraid.

Skeiron: Affiliated Auster territory gang-town.

Silva-Chavez: Affiliated Wespero territory gang-town.

Singh: Affiliated Wespero territory gang-town.

Slip drives: Primary engines used by space-faring ships, which allow them to travel the currents in space.

Sludge: By-product of processed marsanium that is used to fuel the racers on Mars.

Space fish: Slang term for someone who travels space, isn't familiar with planetary life or activities and tends to be impressed easily.

Space hole: Derogatory term, another way to say asshole.

Trolling engine: Engine powered by electricity that works in tandem with a ship's slip drive and can be used inside a planet's atmosphere and when moving short distances.

Uni-rider: Motorcycle-style bike that runs off marsanium sludge.

Upper: Person who lives on an Upper planet.

Upper planets: Jupiter, Saturn and Neptune, including their moons.

Wespero: One of the three territories on Mars.

Zephyr: Affiliated Auster territory gang-town.

Want to see more from this author? Here's a taster for you to enjoy!

Bad Boys of Space: A Talent for Trouble
Landra Graf

Excerpt

The room held the hint of lemons, tropical essence and money. That meant opportunity, and Emilio Morales lived for the next leg up, like having intercepted the invitation to his boss, Manolo, from the Coco Cartel, out of the blue two weeks prior, to meet here on Ganymede at the Chateau Phillipe.

The chateau spanned several acres, with multiple buildings trimmed in gold with tile roofs, fancy materials he'd seen available only to those on the upper planets, not this close to the asteroid belt. Fresh fruit trees in the gardens, fine furniture without holes or tears, guards at every door with automatic weapons, not wheel gun pistols or ceramics. This was what money got a person—whatever they wanted. And Emilio wanted.

Walking in a tight circle, he took in the meeting room. These kinds of fancy surroundings beat the villas and homes of the cartel leaders on Earth by a long shot. Anything was better than sleeping on those hard, wooden cots kept in some drafty room off a main Earth house.

"Do you think they'll feed us any of that?" Emilio asked, motioning to a table behind him. It was covered in sandwiches, fruits, vegetables and a few other more traditional Earth meals, like enchiladas. The last time he'd shoved an enchilada in his mouth had been the day before his partner had offered him a job. Since then, it'd been food cubes, the occasional good meal and plenty of bootlegged booze.

The other group who had received an invitation — a pair of bald-headed men with matching spider tattoos on their hands — stood side-by-side, glancing out of the floor-to-ceiling window. Emilio recognized them as part of the Web Spinners, another drug-runner crew. They mainly worked with cartels in the Western Hemisphere of Earth, whereas Emilio had connections across the globe but did a lot of work in the Eastern Hemisphere.

The skinnier one piped up first. "Feed us? To sharks maybe — did you see that water? Besides, we're here to talk business."

A gong sounded somewhere, echoing through the room. A heavy-set shirtless man, positioned by a white door lined in painted gold roses, announced in a deep bass voice, "The Honorable Alfonso Grecia arrives."

Emilio would normally have shrugged off the elaborate entrance, something he'd seen before during previous business meetings. But, this time, Grecia wasn't doing one-on-one business. He'd opened up to competitors. As the only cartel boss who didn't reside on Earth, choosing to live on the outskirts of the uppers, Grecia was rumored to have ties to Earth royalty from 'before-the-nuke'. Over the years, Emilio's admiration for the man's amassed wealth and power, the way he commanded his organization, had grown. This was something he aspired to have for himself, the reason he'd chosen to attempt putting this deal together on his own...without his cokehead partner.

"Greetings, runners. Join me at my table." Grecia, with his low voice and expressionless face, stood an inch taller than Emilio and wore a floor-length black tunic. He'd already moved to the large cherry-wood table set up in the center of the room and flanked by matching leather upholstered chairs. Damn things even had little rolling wheels on the bottoms, an unexpected, luxurious touch.

Emilio was the last to sit, and Grecia turned his soulless eyes on him. Emilio pushed the gut twinge away, the one that said this man ate bullshitters for breakfast and that Emilio would never get away with his plan.

"Did you have a good trip?" Grecia asked him.

"As expected."

"Why is your partner Manolo not here?"

"He's not allowed on the planet anymore. A disagreement with your local law enforcement." In truth, Manny didn't know anything about this meeting, and nor would he. If all went well, Emilio's mentor might remain in a coke-induced haze while this deal was brokered and executed. "I can speak for both of us."

"Good. Good." The kingpin's attention moved to the Web Spinners, whom he'd ignored so far—possibly a good sign. "And welcome, Recluse. I've brought you both here because I have a proposition for you. My growers have developed a new product called Kiss Kiss. There's nothing like it anywhere on Earth, and I've got buyers waiting on the pleasure moon, Callisto. I don't trust easily and have recently ended my short-term arrangement with the Hermes service."

Hermes had been an established group, with a handful of ships, and according to the latest wire reports, they'd been wiped out. Shot down by law, ships stalled in space with everyone on board dead due to exposure, top lieutenants killed in a poker game gone wrong—the list went on. It appeared Grecia ended things in a permanent fashion. Not a common practice, but accepted if the runners had been acting against their contract.

"You offer us business, but it's not really an offer. More a demand." This crap came from the crossed-armed Recluse in his unexpectedly high-pitched voice, and his skinny, bald companion nodded in agreement.

"What demand? I'm giving you both a chance to prove you're fit to run my exclusive product to the upper planets. If you meet my requirements, then you get this product and all my others. Once I contract with you, my allied cartels will follow suit. You'll control all Eastern Hemisphere running."

Emilio did his best to school his features at Grecia's reply. The benefits and possibilities were too numerous to even list, but the potential to retire from this shit in a matter of months versus years ranked high among them. "What are the requirements?"

Manny would have walked away already, spouting inanities and paranoid theories, whereas Emilio believed in analyzing all facts before making a decision. He hadn't kept their entire enterprise afloat by making half-baked choices.

Grecia smiled and motioned to the man from the door. The lackey dropped a memory disk in the center of the table and up popped a visual projection. It held several images of Earth, Grecia's product and a map. The best part was the way the projection held steady and bright, no fading or flickering, with everything being one hundred percent triggered by touch. A display table almost as good as the ones on Emilio's ship, and a sight better than Manny's.

The drug boss swiped through the images, all smaller versions of what they could be, and selected Earth first. "You'll take your ship to the third planet, retrieve a shipment of my herb, Kiss Kiss, then transport the product to Callisto in six days from receipt."

He selected a map, pulling up the proposed trajectory and fastest route. It took them past all the major hotspots, places runners usually avoided unless they were stupid or suicidal. But the fastest route rode the currents with ease, putting less pressure on a slip drive, using less fuel. Emilio respected Grecia's presentation. It came with a plan.

"If you don't get caught, make it past the checkpoints and no harm comes to the shipment in transit, the contract is yours."

"Ridiculous." Recluse slammed a hand on the table. "No one runs or bootlegs along that route. It's a death trap and a sure-fire way to get your ship and crew pinched."

Attitudes like that get people killed. Emilio piped up fast. "Now, hold up a minute. If His Honorable wants this route run, then his people must know where there may be gaps in security. And if not, my folks would be happy to figure it out. There's nothing like exploring new travel routes." One more lie added to the couple he'd already launched made no difference.

Grecia's mouth twisted. On most people, it would look like a smile, but on his... "I like your thinking. Emilio, right?"

It irked him a bit that the big drug boss knew his partner's name and had to check his, but after this run, he'd make sure this guy always remembered him. They'd be contracted business partners. "That's correct."

"I like your style. You've got—how do they say it on Mars—steel stones?"

"Nuggets, sir. They call 'em steel nuggets."

This provoked a full grin, with teeth this time, and Grecia raised his hand above his head before bringing it down in a forward motion. The visuals on the table disappeared and a slicing sound rent the air. Emilio had been looking at Grecia but heard a gagging sound from the skinny guy and Recluse's head rolled onto the table.

There was no time to react before a blade shoved through Skinny's torso, razor-sharp and lined in red. Emilio took in a steadying breath, low and slow.

"Those men, they have no creativity, no passion. I can tell you do." Grecia walked around the table and sat next to him, steepling his fingers under his chin. "We're going to make this deal between us. You do the job, you deliver the goods and you get all my business."

People died every day, sometimes at his hands. He'd taken lives, almost lost his before. *The nature of the beast, the business.* Emilio could only be thankful his blood wasn't on some assassin's blade. An assassin who'd disappeared into the shadows of the room once more. Staring at Recluse's head, his stomach grumbling with unease, Emilio replied, "Sounds like a plan."

"No." Grecia shook a single finger in the air. "You haven't heard the rest. I determine pricing and you mark up twenty-five percent on this shipment. If you win the business, I'll let you mark up thirty percent."

Emilio whistled low. Yes, the deal wasn't perfect, but no deal was, not in his years of experience. Someone always came out on with the stems on a marijuana plant, as the saying went. But negotiations never got old. "Then I can't guarantee we go the route you want. It's not easy unless there's money to grease the wheels. I have to replace depleted funds."

Markups were always the runner's game, never the cartel's. The cartels made their money on the front end, with the runners assuming all the risk on the backside. That was the way Earth's economy worked. Cartels rarely owned ships, let alone wanted to bring the fury of the United Allied Planets down on them. This boss wanted to change the game—and for what purpose, Emilio didn't need to know. He did need to make sure he earned a profit.

"You, nuggets of steel." Grecia glanced around at his doorman and the guy Emilio hadn't seen, the one responsible for the dead bodies in the room. "Nobody talks to me like this."

"I don't believe in making commitments I can't keep. A man is as good as the deals he honors."

"Have you heard the one about no honor among thieves?" Grecia waved his hand in the air, and two seconds later a door shut behind them. The assassin had been dismissed.

"I'm a runner, not a thief. Soon, the sole runner for the Eastern Hemisphere of Earth."

This made Grecia laugh. A good sign, Emilio hoped.

"I'll tell you what. I'll include twenty-five kilos of Opium Dust and several cases of brandy on the pickup. You sell those and mark them up for whatever you need to cover the expense. I give these to you at cost."

The cost wouldn't do him. Emilio leaned up, propping his elbows on the table. "You give them fifty percent off."

Grecia's smile disappeared. "At cost."

"At cost." He'd settle in order to keep his life and the assassin with his sharp sword out of the room. "Do we shake on it?"

"I don't touch hands, but I'll remember your face, and your ship has already been scanned. Where it goes, I'll know." The boss leaned in close, giving Emilio a good look at the tiny scars running across the older man's cheeks. "If you fuck me over, you won't get the quick treatment disrespectful Recluse received. No, I'll hang you up by your arms and ensure you die slow. Now, let's eat."

About the Author

Landra Graf consumes at least one book a day, and has always been a sucker for stories where true love conquers all. She believes in the power of the written word, and the joy such words can bring. In between spending time with her family and having book adventures, she writes romance with the goal of giving everyone, fictional or not, their own happily ever after.

Landra loves to hear from readers. You can find her contact information, website details and author profile page at https://www.totallybound.com

Home of Erotic Romance

Sign up for our newsletter and find out about all our romance book releases, eBook sales and promotions, sneak peeks and FREE romance books!

www.ingramcontent.com/pod-product-compliance
Lightning Source LLC
Chambersburg PA
CBHW020824260626
47169CB00003B/815